The Wolves of
Willoughby Chase

YOUNG AMERICA BOOK CLUB

A Division of Weekly Reader Children's Book Club

Presents

The Wolves of Willoughby Chase

By JOAN AIKEN

Illustrated by PAT MARRIOTT

DOUBLEDAY & COMPANY, INC.
GARDEN CITY, NEW YORK

For
JOHN *and* ELIZABETH *and*
TORQUEMADA

One

It was dusk—winter dusk. Snow lay white and shining over the pleated hills, and icicles hung from the forest trees. Snow lay piled on the dark road across Willoughby Wold, but from dawn men had been clearing it with brooms and shovels. There were hundreds of them at work, wrapped in sacking because of the bitter cold, and keeping together in groups for fear of the wolves, grown savage and reckless from hunger.

Snow lay thick, too, upon the roof of Willoughby Chase, the great house that stood on an open eminence in the heart of the wold. But for all that, the Chase looked an inviting home—a warm and welcoming stronghold. Its rosy herringbone brick was bright and well-cared-for, its numerous turrets and battlements stood up sharp against the sky, and the crenelated balconies, corniced with snow, each held a golden square of window. The house was all alight within, and the joyous hubbub of its activity contrasted with the somber sighing of the wind and the hideous howling of the wolves without.

In the nursery a little girl was impatiently dancing up

and down before the great window, fourteen feet high, which faced out over the park and commanded the long black expanse of road.

"Will she be here soon, Pattern? Will she?" was her continual cry.

"We shall hear soon enough, I dare say, Miss Bonnie," was the inevitable reply from her maid, who, on hands and knees in front of the fire, was folding and goffering the frills of twenty lace petticoats.

The little girl turned again to her impatient vigil. She had climbed up on to the window seat, the better to survey the snowy park, and was jumping on its well-sprung cushions, covered in crimson satin. Each time she bounced, she nearly hit the ceiling.

"Give over, Miss Bonnie, do," said Pattern after a while. "Look at the dust you're raising. I can hardly see my tongs. Come and sit by the fire. We shall hear soon enough when the train's due."

Bonnie left her perch reluctantly enough and came to sit by the fire. She was a slender creature, small for her age, but rosy-cheeked, with a mass of tumbled black locks falling to her shoulders, and two brilliant blue eyes, equally ready to dance with laughter or flash with indignation. Her square chin also gave promise of a powerful and obstinate temper, not always perfectly controlled. But her mouth was sweet, and she could be very thoughtful on occasion—as now, when she sat gazing into the fire, piled high on its two carved alabaster wolfhounds.

"I hope the train hasn't been delayed by wolves," she said presently.

"*Nonsense*, Miss Bonnie dear—don't worry your pretty head with thoughts like that," replied Pattern. "You know the porters and stationmaster have been practicing with their muskets and fowling pieces all the week."

At that moment there was a commotion from downstairs, and Bonnie turned, her face alight with expectancy. As the noise of dogs barking, men shouting, and the doorbell clanging continued, she flew recklessly along the huge expanse of nursery floor, gleaming and polished as glass, and down the main staircase to the entrance hall. Her impetuosity brought her in a heep to the feet of an immensely tall, thin lady, clad from neck to toe in a traveling dress of swathed gray twill, with a stiff collar, dark glasses, and dull green buttoned boots. Bonnie's headlong rush nearly sent this person flying, and she recovered her blance with an exclamation of annoyance.

"Who is guilty of this unmannerly irruption?" she said, settling her glasses once more upon her nose. "Can this hoydenish creature be my new pupil?"

"I—I beg your pardon!" Bonnie exclaimed, picking herself up.

"So I should hope! Am I right in supposing that you are Miss Green? I am Miss Slighcarp, your new governess. I am also your fourth cousin, once removed," the lady added haughtily, as if she found the removal hardly sufficient.

"Oh," Bonnie stammered, "I didn't know—that is, I thought you were not expected until tomorrow. I was looking for my cousin Sylvia, who is arriving this evening."

"I am aware of the fact," Miss Slighcarp replied coldly, "but that does not excuse bad manners. Where, pray, is your curtsy?"

"Rather flustered, Bonnie performed this formality with less than her usual grace.

"Lessons in deportment, I see, will need priority on our timetable," Miss Slighcarp remarked, and she turned to look after the disposition of her luggage. "You, sir! Do not stand there smirking and dawdling, but see that my valises are

9

carried at once to my apartments, and that my maid is immediately in attendance to help me."

James, the footman, who had been exchanging grimaces with the butler over the fact that he had received no tip, at once sprang to attention, and said:

"Your maid, miss? Did you bring a maid with you?"

"No, blockhead. The maid whom Lady Green will have appointed to wait on me."

"Well, I suppose Miss Pattern will be helping you," said James, scratching his head, and he shouldered one of the nine walrus-hide portmanteaux and staggered off to the service stairs.

"I will show you the way to your room," said Bonnie eagerly, "and when you are ready I will take you to see Papa and Mamma. I hope we shall love each other," she continued, leading the way up the magnificent marble staircase, and along the portrait gallery. "I shall have so much to show you—my collection of flint arrowheads and my semi-precious stones."

Miss Slighcarp thinned her lips disapprovingly and Bonnie, fearing that she had been forward, said no more of her pursuits.

"Here is your apartment," she explained presently, opening a door and exhibiting a commodious set of rooms, cheerful with fires and furnished with elegant taste in gilt and mahogany. "And here is my maid Pattern to help you."

Miss Slighcarp drew down her brows at this, but acknowledged the remark by an inclination of her head. Pattern was already kneeling at the dressing case and drawing out such articles as the governess might immediately need.

"I shall leave you, then, for the moment," said Bonnie, preparing to go. She turned to add, "Shall I come back in half an hour?" but was arrested by the sight of Miss Slighcarp snatching a heavy marble hairbrush from its rest and striking a savage blow at the maid, who had taken out a little case apparently containing letters and papers.

"Prying wretch! Who gave you permission to meddle with my letters?" she cried.

Bonnie sprang back in an instant, all her violent temper roused, and seized the brush from Miss Slighcarp's hand, hurling it recklessly through the plate-glass window. She picked up a jug of warm water which a housemaid had just brought, and dashed it full in the face of her new instructress.

Miss Slighcarp reeled under the impact—her bonnet came off, so did her gray hair, which, apparently, was a wig, leaving her bald, dripping, and livid with rage.

"Oh dear—I am so sorry!" said Bonnie in consternation. "I did not mean to do that. My temper is a dreadful fault. But you must not strike Pattern. She is one of my best friends. Oh Pattern—help her!"

The maid assisted Miss Slighcarp to replace the damp wig and repair the damage done by the water, but her compressed lips and nostrils showed how little she relished the task. An angry red weal was rising on her cheek where the brush had struck her.

"Go!" said Miss Slighcarp to Bonnie, pointing at the door.

Bonnie was glad to do so. Half an hour later, though, she returned, having done her best in the meantime to wrestle with her rebellious temper.

"Shall I escort you to Mamma and Papa now?" she said, when the governess bade her enter. Miss Slighcarp had changed into another gray twill dress with a high white collar, and had laid aside her merino traveling cloak.

She permitted Bonnie to lead her toward the apartments of her parents, having first locked up several drawers in which she had deposited papers, and placed the keys in a chatelaine at her belt.

Bonnie, whose indignation never lasted long, danced ahead cheerfully enough, pointing out to her companion the oubliette where Cousin Roger had slipped, the panel which concealed a secret staircase, the haunted portico, the priests' hole, and other features of her beloved home. Miss Slighcarp, however, as she followed, wore on her face an expression that boded little good toward her charge.

At length they paused before a pair of doors grander than any they had yet passed, and Bonnie inquired of the attendant who stood before them if her parents were within. Receiving an affirmative answer, she joyfully entered and, running toward an elegant-looking lady and gentleman who were seated on an ottoman near the fireplace, exclaimed:

"Papa! Mamma! Such a surprise! Here is Miss Slighcarp, come a day earlier than expected!"

Miss Slighcarp advanced and made her salutations to her employers.

"I regret not having come up to London to make arrangements with you myself," said Sir Willoughby, bowing easily to her, "but my good friend and man of business Mr. Gripe will have told you how we are situated—on the eve of a departure, with so much to attend to. I had been aware that we had a distant cousin—yourself, ma'am—living in London, and I entrusted Mr. Gripe with the task of seeking you out and asking whether you would be willing to undertake the care of my estates and my child while we are abroad. My only other relative, my sister Jane, is as perhaps you know, too frail and elderly for such a responsibility. I hope you and Bonnie will get on together famously."

Here Miss Slighcarp, in a low and grating tone, told him the story of the hairbrush and the jug of water, omitting, however, her unprovoked assault in the first place upon poor Pattern. Sir Willoughby burst into laughter.

"Did she do that, the minx? Eh, you hussy!" and he lovingly pinched his daughter's cheek. "Girls will be girls, Miss Slighcarp, and you must allow something for the natural high spirits and excitement attendant on your own arrival and the expected one of her cousin. I shall look to you to instill, in time, a more ladylike deportment into our wild sprite."

Lady Green, who was dark-haired and sad-eyed, and who looked very ill, here raised her voice wearily and asked her husband if that were not a knock on the door. He called a summons impatiently, and the stationmaster entered—a black, dingy figure, twisting his cap in his hands.

"The down train is signaled, Squire," he said, after bobbing his head in reverence to each of the persons present in the room. "Is it your pleasure to let it proceed?"

"Surely, surely," said Sir Willoughby. "My little niece is aboard it—let it approach with all speed. How did you come from the station, my man? Walked? Let orders be given for Solly to drive you back in the chaise—with a suitable escort, of course—then he can wait there and bring back Miss Sylvia at the same time."

"Oh, thank you indeed, sir," said the man with heartfelt gratitude. "Bless your noble heart! It would have taken me a weary while to walk those ten miles back, and it is freezing fast."

"That's all right," said Sir Willoughby heartily. "Mustn't let Miss Sylvia die of cold on the train. Besides, the wolves might get you, and then the poor child would be held up on the train all night for want of the signal. Never do, eh? Well, Bonnie, what is it, miss?"

"Oh, Papa," said Bonnie, who had been plucking at his

sleeve, "may I go with Solly in the chaise to meet Sylvia? May I?"

"No indulgence should be permitted a child who has behaved as she has done," remarked Miss Slighcarp.

"Oh, come, come, Miss Slighcarp, come, come, ma'am," said Sir Willoughby good-naturedly. "Young blood, you know. Besides, my Bonnie's as good a shot at a wolf as any of them. Run along, then, miss, but wrap up snug—remember you'll be several hours on the road."

"Oh, thank you, Papa! Goodbye! Goodbye, Mamma dear, goodbye, Miss Slighcarp!" and she fondly kissed her parents and ran from the room to find her warmest bonnet and pelisse.

"Reckless, foolish indulgence," muttered the governess, directing after Bonnie a look of the purest spite.

"But hey!" exclaimed Sir Willoughby, recalled to memory of Miss Slighcarp's presence by the sound though he missed the sense, of her words. "If the train's only just signaled, how did you come, then, ma'am? You can't have flown here, hey?"

For the first time the governess showed signs of confusion.

"I—er—that is to say, a friend who was driving over from Blastburn kindly offered to bring me here with my baggage," she at length replied.

A bell clanged through the apartment at that moment.

"The dressing bell," said Sir Willoughby, looking at a handsome gold watch, slung on a chain across his ample waistcoat. "I apprehend, Miss Slighcarp, that you are fatigued from your journey and will not wish to dine with us. A meal will be served in your own apartments."

He inclined his head in a dignified gesture of dismissal, which the governess had no option but to obey.

Two

Two days before these events a very different scene had been enacted far away in London, where Bonnie's cousin Sylvia was being prepared for her journey.

Sylvia was an orphan, both her parents having been carried off by a fever when she was only an infant. She lived with her Aunt Jane, who was now becoming very aged and frail and had written to Sir Willoughby to suggest that he took on the care of the little girl. He had agreed at once to this proposal, for Sylvia, he knew, was delicate, and the country air would do her good. Besides, he welcomed the idea of her gentle companionship for his rather harum-scarum Bonnie.

Aunt Jane and Sylvia shared a room at the top of a house. It was in Park Lane, this being the only street in which Aunt Jane could consider living. Unfortunately, as she was very poor, she could afford to rent only a tiny attic in such a genteel district. The room was divided into two by a very beautiful, but old, curtain of white Chinese brocade. She and Sylvia each had half the room at night, Aunt Jane sleeping on the divan and Sylvia on the ottoman. During the daytime the curtain was drawn back and hung elegantly looped against the wall. They cooked their meals over the gas jet, and had baths in a large enameled Chinese bowl, covered with dragons, an heirloom of Aunt Jane's.

At other times it stood on a little occasional table by the door and was used for visiting cards.

They were making Sylvia's clothes.

Aunt Jane, with tears running down her face, had taken down the white curtain (which would no longer be needed) and was cutting it up. Fortunately it was large enough to afford material for several chemises, petticoats, pantalettes, dresses, and even a bonnet. Aunt Jane, mopping her eyes with a tiny shred of the material, murmured:

"I do like to see a little girl dressed all in white."

"I *wish* we needn't cut up your curtain, Auntie, "said Sylvia, who hated to see her aunt so distressed. "When I'm thirty-five and come into my money, I shall buy you a whole set of white brocade curtains."

"There's my angel," her aunt replied, embracing her. "But when you are thirty-five I shall be a hundred and three," and she set to work making the tucks in a petticoat with thousands of tiny stitches. Sylvia sighed, and bent her fair head over another, with stitches almost equally tiiny. She was a little depressed—though she would not dream of saying so—at the idea of wearing nothing but white, especially at her cousin Bonnie's, where everything was sure to be grand and handsome.

"Now let me think," muttered Aunt Jane, sewing away like lightning. "What can we use to make you a traveling cloak?"

She paused for a moment and glanced round the room, at the lovingly tended pieces of Sheraton and Hepplewhite furniture, the antimacassars, the Persian screen across the gas-jet kitchen. The window curtains were too threadbare to use—and in any case one must have window curtains. At last she recollected an old green velvet shawl which they sometimes used as an extra bedcover when it was very cold and they slept together on the ottoman.

"I can use my jet-trimmed mantle instead," she said reassuringly to Sylvia. "After all, one person cannot be so cold as two."

By the day of departure, all the clothes had been finished. Nothing much could be done about Sylvia's shoes, which were deplorably shabby, but Aunt Jane blacked them with a mixture of soot and candle grease, and Sylvia's bonnet was trimmed with a white plume from the ostrich-feather fan which her aunt had carried at her coming-out ball. All Sylvia's belongings were neatly packed into an old carpet-bag, and Aunt Jane had made her up a little packet of provisions for the journey, though with strict injunctions not to eat them if there were anyone else in the compartment.

"For ladies *never* eat in public."

They were too poor to take a hackney carriage to the station, and Aunt Jane always refused to travel in omnibuses, so they walked, carrying the bag between them. Fortunately the station was not far, nor the bag heavy.

Aunt Jane secured a corner seat for her charge, and put her under the care of the guard.

"Now remember, my dear child," she said, kissing Sylvia and looking suspiciously round the empty compartment, "never speak to strangers, tip all the servants immediately (I have put all the farthings from my reticule at the bottom of your valise); do not model yourself on your cousin Bonnie, who I believe is a dear good child but a little wild; give my fond regards to my brother Willoughby and tell him that I am in the pink of health and *amply* provided for; and if anyone except the guard speaks to you, pull the communication cord."

"Yes, Auntie," replied Sylvia dutifully, embracing her. She felt a pang as she saw the frail old figure struggling away through the crowd, and wondered how her Aunt Jane would manage that evening without her little niece to adjust her curlpapers and read aloud a page of Dr. Johnson's Dictionary.

Then all Sylvia's fears were aroused, for a strange man entered the compartment and sat down. He did not speak, however, and took no notice of her, and, the train shortly afterward departing, her thoughts were diverted into a less apprehensive vein as she watched the unfamiliar houses with their lighted windows flying past.

It was to be a long journey—a night and a day. The hour of departure was six o'clock in the evening, and Sylvia knew that she did not arrive at her destination until about eight of the following evening. What strange forests, towns, mountains, and stretches of countryside would they not have passed by then, as the train proceeded at its steady fifteen miles an hour! She had never been out of London before, and watched eagerly from her window until they had left the houses behind, and she was driven to study the toes of her own shoes, so lovingly polished by Aunt Jane.

The thought of the old lady, carefully preparing for her solitary slumbers, was too much for Sylvia, and tears began to run silently down her cheeks, which she endeavored to mop with her tiny handkerchief (made from a spare two inches of white brocade).

"Here, this won't do," said a voice in her ear suddenly, and she looked up in alarm to see that the man at the other end of the compartment had moved along and was sitting opposite and staring at her. Sylvia gave her eyes a final dab and haughtily concentrated on her reflection in the dark window, but her heart was racing. Should she pull the communication cord? She stole a cautious glance at the man's reflection and saw that he was standing up, apparently extracting something from a large leather port-manteau. Then he turned toward her, holding something out: she looked round enough to see that it was a box of chocolates about a foot square by six inches deep, swathed around with violet ribbons.

"No, thank you," said Sylvia, in as ladylike a tone as she could muster. "I never touch chocolate." All the same, she had to swallow rapidly a couple of times, for the tea which she had shared with Aunt Jane before the journey, although very refined, had not been substantial—two pieces of thin bread-and-butter, a cinnamon wafer, and a sliver of caraway cake.

She knew better, however, than to accept food from strangers, and as to opening her own little packet while he was in the carriage—that was out of the question. She shook her head again.

"Now come along—do," said the man coaxingly. "All little girls like sweeties, *I* know."

"Sir," said Sylvia coldly, "if you speak to me again I shall be obliged to pull the communication cord."

He sighed and put away the box. Her relief over this was premature, however, for he turned round next minute with a confectioners' pasteboard carton filled with every imaginable variety of little cakes—there were jam tarts, maids of honor, lemon cheese cakes, Chelsea buns, and numerous little iced confections in brilliant and enticing colors.

"I always put up a bit of tiffin for a journey," he murmured as if to himself, and, placing the box on the seat directly opposite Sylvia, he selected a cake covered with violet icing and bit into it. It appeared to be filled with jam. Sylvia looked straight ahead and ignored him, but again she had to swallow.

"Now my dear, how about one of these little odds and ends?" said the man. "I can't possibly eat them all by myself—can I?"

Sylvia stood up and looked for the communication cord. It was out of her reach.

"Shall I pull it for you?" inquired her fellow traveler politely, following the direction of her eyes upward. Sylvia did not reply to him. She did not feel, though, that it would be ladylike to climb up on the seat or armrest to pull the cord herself, so she sat down again, biting her lip with anxiety. To her inexpressible relief the stranger, after eating three or four more cakes with every appearance of enjoyment, put the box back in his portmanteau, wrapped himself in a richly furred cloak, retired to his own corner, and shut his eyes. A subdued but regular snore soon issuing from his partly opened mouth presently convinced Sylvia that he was asleep, and she began to breathe more freely. At length she brought out from concealment under her mantle her most treasured possession, and held it lovingly in her arms.

This was a doll named Annabelle, made of wood, not much larger than a candle, and plainly dressed, but extremely dear to Sylvia. She and Annabelle had no secrets from one another, and it was a great comfort to her to have this companion as the train rocked on through the unfamiliar dark.

Presently she grew drowsy and fell into uneasy slumber, but not for long; it was bitterly cold and her feet in their thin shoes felt like lumps of ice. She huddled into her corner and wrapped herself in the green cloak, envying her companion his thick furs and undisturbed repose, and wishing it were ladylike to curl her feet up beneath her on the seat. Unfortunately she knew better than that.

She dreamed, without being really asleep, of arctic seas, of monstrous tunnels through hillsides fringed with icicles. Her traveling companion, who had grown a long tail and a pair of horns, offered her cakes the size of grand pianos and colored scarlet, blue, and green; when she bit into them she found they were made of snow.

She woke suddenly from one of these dreams to find that the train had stopped with a jerk.

"Oh! What is it? Where are we?" she exclaimed before she could stop herself.

"No need to alarm yourself, miss," said her companion, looking unavailingly out of the black square of window. "Wolves on the line, most likely—they often have trouble of that kind hereabouts."

"Wolves!" Sylvia stared at him in terror.

"They don't often get into the train, though," he added reassuringly. "Two years ago they managed to climb into

the guard's van and eat a pig, and once they got the engine driver—another had to be sent in a relief engine—but they don't often eat a passenger, I promise you."

As if in contradiction of his words a sad and sinister howling now arose beyond the windows, and Sylvia, pressing her face against the dark pane, saw that they were passing through a thickly wooden region where snow lay deep on the ground. Across this white carpet she could just discern a ragged multitude pouring, out of which arose, from time to time, this terrible cry. She was almost petrified with fear and sat clutching Annabelle in a cold and trembling hand. At length she summoned up strength to whisper:

"Why don't we go on?"

"Oh, I expect there are too many of 'em on the line ahead," the man answered carelessly. "Can't just push through them, you see—the engine would be derailed in no time, and then we *should* be in a bad way. No, I expect we'll have to wait here till daylight now—the wolves get scared then, you know, and make for home. All that matters is that the driver shan't get eaten in the meantime—he'll keep 'em off by throwing lumps of coal at them I dare say."

"Oh!" Sylvia exclaimed in irrepressible alarm, as a heavy body thudded suddenly against the window, and she had a momentary view of a pointed gray head, red slavering jaws, and pale eyes gleaming with ferocity.

"Oh, don't worry about that," soothed her companion. "They'll keep up that jumping against the windows for hours. They're not much danger, you know, singly; it's only in the whole pack you've got to watch out for 'em."

Sylvia was not much comforted by this. She moved along to the middle of the seat and huddled there, glancing fearfully first to one side and then to the other. The strange man seemed quite undisturbed by the repeated onslaught of the wolves which followed. He took a pinch of snuff, remarked that it was all a great nuisance and they would be late, and composed himself to sleep again.

He had just begun to snore when a discomposing incident occurred. The window beside him, which must have been insecurely fastened, was not proof against the continuous impact of the frenzied and ravenous animals. The catch suddenly slipped, and the window fell open with a crash, its glass shivering into fragments.

Sylvia screamed. Another instant, and a wolf precipitated itself through the aperture thus formed. It turned snarling on the sleeping stranger, who started awake with an oath, and very adroitly flung his cloak over the animal. He then seized one of the shattered pieces of glass lying on the floor and stabbed the imprisoned beast through the cloak. It fell dead.

"Tush," said Sylvia's companion, breathing heavily and passing his hand over his face. "Unexpected—most."

He extracted the dead wolf from the folds of the cloak and tipped its body, with some exertion, out through the broken window. There was a chorus of snarling and yelping outside, and then the wolves seemed to take fright at the appearance of their dead comrade, for Sylvia saw them coursing away over the snow.

"Come, that's capital," said the man. "We'd better shift before they come back."

"Shift?"

"Into another compartment," he explained. "Can't stay in this one now—too cold for one thing, and for another, have wolves popping in the whole time—nuisance. No, come along, now's the time to do it."

Sylvia was most reluctant, and indeed almost too terrified to accompany him, but she saw the force of his proposal and watched anxiously as he opened the door and glanced this way and that.

"Right! Just pass me out those bags, will you?" He had placed both his and hers ready on the seat. She passed them out. Holding them in one hand, he made his way sideways along the footboard to the next carriage door, which he opened. He tossed in the bags, returned for his cloak and rug, and finally reappeared and held out his hand to Sylvia.

"Come along now, my dear, if you don't want to be made into wolf porridge," he exclaimed with frightening joviality, and Sylvia timorously permitted him to assist her along the narrow ledge and into the next carriage. It was with a sense of unbounded relief and thankfulness that she heard him slam the door and make sure that the windows were securely fastened.

"Excellent," he remarked with a smile at Sylvia which bared every tooth in his head. "Now we can have another forty winks," and he wrapped himself up again in his cloak, careless of any wolf gore that might remain on its folds, and shut his eyes.

Sylvia was too cold and terrified to sleep. She crouched, as before, in the middle of the seat—icy, shivering, and expecting at any minute to hear the wolves recommence their attack against the window.

"Here, we can't have this," said a disapproving voice, and she turned to see the man awake again and scrutinizing her closely. "Not warm enough, eh? Here . . ." and then as he saw her wince away from his cloak, he unstrapped a warm plaid traveling rug and insisted on wrapping her in it. Tired, frozen, and frightened, Sylvia was unable to resist him any longer.

"Put your feet up and lie down," he ordered. "That's right. Now shut your eyes. No more wolves for the time being—they've been scared away. Off to sleep with you."

Sylvia was beginning to be deliciously warm. Her last recollection was of hearing his snores begin again.

Three

When Sylvia woke, it was broad daylight and the train was running through a mountainous region, wooded here and there, and with but few and scattered dwellings. Her companion was already awake, and munching away at an enormous piece of cold sausage.

Sylvia felt herself to be nearly dead of hunger. She remembered Aunt Jane's precept, "Never eat in front of strangers," but surely Aunt Jane had not intended her to go for a whole night and a day without taking *some* refreshment? And moreover, the good soul could not have anticipated the dreadful perils that her niece was to encounter, perils which had left Sylvia so weak and faint that she felt she might never reach Willoughby Chase alive unless she could open her little packet and consume some of its contents. Perhaps, she thought, the shared adventure of the wolves formed some sort of an introduction to her fellow traveler.

She pondered over this matter for some time and at length, driven by her ravenous appetite, and with many timorous glances at the strange man, she opened her carpet-bag and took from her parcel of food one or two of the little dry rolls her aunt had provided—rolls that contained in each a tiny sliver of ham, frail and thin as pink tissue paper. The remainder she put back for later in the day. After this frugal meal she felt greatly restored, and was not too discomposed when she saw that the man, having devoured his sausage down to the twisted end, was now smiling at her in a manner that was evidently intended to be the height of amiability.

"There! Now we both feel better," he remarked.

"It was most kind of you, sir, to lend me your rug," Sylvia faltered.

"Couldn't let you freeze to death, m'dear, could I? Not after you'd shown such pluck and spirit over the wolves. Some little gels would have screamed and cried, I can tell you!"

"Will they come back again?" inquired Sylvia, glancing anxiously out. The train was now running across a wide snowy plain, dazzlingly bright under the sun of a clear blue morning.

"Not till this evening," he told her. "When we get to the wolds at dusk you can depend on it there'll be wolves there to meet us. No need to worry, though."

Sylvia looked her doubt of this statement, and he exclaimed, "Pshaw! Wolves are cowardly brutes! They won't hurt you unless they outnumber you by more than ten to one. If you feel anxious about it I'll get my gun, though I don't generally use it for small fry."

And to Sylvia's alarm he pulled down a canvas-wrapped bundle that she had taken for fishing rods and took from it a long, heavy, glinting blue gun. Opening a smaller bag he brought out a few cartridges and clapped them into the breech. Then, turning to Sylvia—she winced away in alarm —he said, "Now, my dear, shall I give you a proof of my marksmanship? Shall I, eh?"

"Oh, no, sir, please don't! Please do not! Indeed, indeed, I am sure you can shoot extremely well!"

"Can't be sure till you have seen me! And it will pass the time for us both."

So saying, he opened the window at one end of the compartment while Sylvia, with her hands to her ears, pressed herself as far as possible into a corner at the other end.

"Now then, what's there to shoot. Can't very well shoot cattle, though it would be a rare joke, ha ha! There's a bunny, bang! Got him—did you see him go head over heels?" Sylvia had seen no such thing, for her hands were over her eyes, and her nose buried in the red-and-black patterned upholstery.

"Now a rook—he's flapping along slowly, I'll wait till we catch him up—there! Tumbled down like a stone. The farmer'll wonder where he came from."

He fired one or two more shots and then remarked, "But I mustn't waste all my cartridges, must keep some for the wolves, what?" and put the gun back in its case, carefully cleaning it before he did so. The compartment was reeking with acrid blue smoke and Sylvia was nearly choking.

"There, I never asked if you'd like to try a shot," the man said, "but I fancy the gun would be a bit heavy for you, as you're on the small side—a lighter fowling piece would be the thing for you."

"Indeed, I hope I shall never need to shoot at all," said Sylvia, horrified at the very possibility of such an idea.

"Never know when it might come in useful—my old mother used to say that every little girl should be able to cook, play the piano, sing, and shoot."

Sylvia thought of Aunt Jane's very different catalogue of accomplishments for little girls, in which crewel work, purse netting, and making paper doilies took high place, and could not agree with him. The thought of Aunt Jane made her sad once more and she sighed deeply.

"Are you going far?" the man asked. "Let's get acquainted. My name's Grimshaw—Josiah Grimshaw."

Sylvia did not much wish to confide in him, but she felt that if she did not talk to him he might get bored and recommence shooting out of the window. Anything was preferable to that. Accordingly she told him her name, and that she was traveling to the house of her uncle, Sir Willoughby Green.

He expressed great interest in this.

"Ah yes, yes indeed. I've heard of Sir Willoughby. Richest man in five counties, isn't he?"

Sylvia knew nothing of that.

"And you'll have a fine time there, eh? Shall you be staying there long?"

"Oh yes. You see, my dear mamma and papa are dead, and so I am to live there now with my cousin Bonnie."

"And your uncle and aunt will look after you," he said, nodding.

"Oh, not for very long," she told him. "My poor Aunt Sophia is very delicate, and it is necessary for my uncle to take her on a voyage south for her health, so they will be leaving very soon after I get there. My poor cousin Bonnie, how she will miss them! But we shall have a governess who is related to us, and of course there are many servants there to look after us. And I hope that Aunt Sophy will soon be better and come back to England—Aunt Jane says that she is so pretty and kind!"

He nodded again.

Afternoon was now come upon them—gray, with promise of more snow. The train had left the levels and was running into more upland country—waste, wide, and lonely, with not a living thing stirring across its bare and open expanses. It was bleak and forbidding, and Sylvia shivered a little, thinking what a long way there was yet to go before she reached her unknown destination.

The day dragged on. To her relief Mr. Grimshaw presently fell asleep again and sat snoring in his corner. Sylvia took out Annabelle once more and showed her the landscape—it seemed to her that the poor doll looked somewhat startled and dismayed at the dreary prospect, which was not surprising, since her painted eyes had never before surveyed anything wilder than Hyde Park on a sunny morning.

"Never mind, Annabelle," Sylvia said, comforting her, "we'll be there soon, and there will be warm fires and many beautiful things to look at. I expect Bonnie will have many doll-friends for you to play with. Oh dear, I only hope they won't laugh at you in your funny little old pelisse!"

She felt rather self-reproachful about Annabelle's old clothes, but there really had not been a scrap of the white curtain left by the time her own outfit had been completed. She consoled herself and the doll as best she could, and presently sang some quiet songs in an undertone when it seemed fairly sure, judging by the loudness of Mr. Grimshaw's snores, that she would not wake him with her singing.

At length darkness came, and poor Sylvia was dismayed by the sight, while it was yet dusk, of many animal shapes streaming in a broken formation across the snow. She heard again that lonely, heart-shaking cry of the wolves and wondered whether to waken Mr. Grimshaw and tell him.

But the train chugged on its way without slowing, and the wolves came and went in the shadows of the trees, never approaching very near, so that she felt it would be cowardly to disturb him, and as long as there was no immediate danger she greatly preferred to let him sleep on.

It was now quite dark, and Sylvia wished very much that she had some means of knowing the time. Mr. Grimshaw had a great gold watch in his waistcoat, but this was covered up, and she could not tell whether she was likely soon to reach her journey's end. She had been in readiness since twilight, with the last little hard roll eaten and the carpet-bag buckled up, and Annabelle safety tucked away under her cloak once more.

All at once there was a grinding jerk and the train came

with violent abruptness to a halt, the wheels screeching in protest and the windows almost starting from their frames.

"Oh, what has happened? What can it be?" cried Sylvia.

Mr. Grimshaw leaped to his feet and reached upward to pull down his portmanteau from the rack. But either from clumsiness or on account of the jolt with which the next coach struck theirs as it slid to a halt, he gave the case too vigorous a tug. It topped forward and fell with a most appalling crash directly upon his head, felling him to the floor. He lay apparently stunned.

Sylvia was terrified. She sat utterly fixed for two or three seconds, and then rushed to the window, which had fallen open when the train stopped, and thrust out her head to see if there was anyone to whom she might appeal for help.

Greatly to her relief and joy, she discovered that they had actually stopped at a little forest station. Her portion of the train was at the extreme end of the platform, and the wildly swinging and flickering lamps did not enable her to read the name upon the notice board, but she saw that a little group of persons carrying lamps and bundles were rapidly approaching down the length of the station, appearing to glance into each compartment in turn as they proceeded. She could not distinguish individuals of the group, but gathered an impression of urgency from their manner, an impression which was intensified by some indistinguishable shouts from the engine driver, borne back on the wind.

"Help!" called Sylvia, leaning from her window. "Help, please!"

She was afraid that her faint cry would not be heard, but at least one member of the group responded to it, for there was an answering halloo, and a small figure detached itself from the rest and darted forward.

"Sylvia! Is it you?"

Sylvia had hardly time to register more than a pair of bright, dark eyes, rosy cheeks, black locks escaping from under a little fur cap, before with a cry of "Mind, now, Miss Bonnie, don't get so far ahead!" a man had come up and was busy undoing the fastening of the compartment door.

"Miss Sylvia, is it, miss? We'll soon have you out of there," he called cheerily, wrestling with the frozen and snow-covered handle, while Bonnie somewhat impeded his activities, dancing up and down, blowing kisses to Sylvia, and crying, "Poor dear Sylvia, you must be frozen! Never mind, you'll soon be warm and snug, we have a foot warmer and ever so many blankets in the carriage. Oh, how I am going to love you! What fun we shall have!"

Sylvia responded heartily to these overtures, and then exclaimed urgently to the man, who had now undone the door, "There is a gentleman here in need of assistance. I greatly fear that he has been stunned by his suitcase. Pray, pray, can you help him?"

"Let's have a look at him, then, miss," the man said. "You pop out with Miss Bonnie and let James take you back to the carriage. That will be safest for you."

But Bonnie exclaimed, all interest, "A man hurt? Oh, the poor fellow! We must help him, Solly. We had better take him home."

The other members of the group had come up by now, and there was clamor and discussion.

"What's to be done? Can't leave the poor gentleman in the train like that, 'tis another two hours to Blastburn and like as not he'd freeze to death."

"Well, whatever you do," said a whiskered man in a flat cap who appeared to be the stationmaster, "do it quick, or the wolves'll settle the matter. Hark, I hear them now! We've

not a moment to spare." And an anxious toot from the
engine driver's whistle seemed to indicate that he was likewise of this opinion.

"Take him out, then," cried Bonnie, "put him in the carriage! I am sure my father would wish it." And James
and Solly agreeing, Mr. Grimshaw and his luggage were
lifted forth, together with Sylvia's carpetbag, the door was
slammed, and the guard waved his green lamp. Smoke and
sparks puffed back on the wind as the engine heaved itself
under way and the train slowly ground forward, the guard
nimbly swung himself on board as the rear of the train
passed them, and Sylvia, glancing back as she was hurried
along the platform by Bonnie's eager hand, saw its serpent
line of lights disappear winding through the trees. Now the
grinding and hissing of the engine was gone, Sylvia could

hear the howls of wolves, distinct and frightening, and she understood the haste of the party to be gone.

She received a confused impression of the small station building, with its fringed canopy and scarlet-painted seats, as she was hustled through, and then they came to the neat little carriage in front of which six black horses were steaming, stamping, and shivering under their rugs, as impatient as the humans to be off.

"Lay him on the seat!" cried Bonnie. "That's it, James! Now wrap a rug over him, so—is his luggage all there? Capital. Now Sylvia, spring in!" But poor Sylvia was too exhausted and cold to manage it, and James the footman lifted her carefully up and deposited her on the opposite seat, wrapping her in a beautiful soft blue merino rug and placing her feet upon a foot warmer. Bonnie snuggled in beside her and cried, "Now we can go!"

And indeed, it was only just in time. As James and Solly swung themselves up and the station staff dashed inside their little edifice, there was a chorus of yelps and howls, and the first of a considerable pack of wolves came loping into the station yard. There was a flash and a deafening report as James fired his musket among them. Solly whipped up the horses, who needed no whipping, and the carriage seemed almost to spring off the ground, so rapid was the motion with which it left the building and lights behind.

There had been a new fall of snow and their progress was silent as they flew over the carpeted ground, save for the muffled hoofbeats and the cry of the wolves behind them.

"Those poor men in the station!" exclaimed Sylvia. "Will they be safe?"

"Oh yes," Bonnie told her reassuringly. "They have plenty of ammunition. We always bring them some when we come, and food too—and the wolves can't get in. It's only troublesome when a train has to stop and people get out. But tell me about that poor man—what is the matter with him? Was he taken ill?"

"No, it was his portmanteau that fell on him and knocked him unconscious," Sylvia explained. "The train stopped with such a jerk."

"Yes, the drivers always do that. You see, if the wolves notice a train slowing down, they are on the alert at once, and all start to run toward the station, so as to be there when the passengers get out. Consequently, if a train has to stop here, the driver goes as fast as he can till the very last moment, in order to deceive them into thinking that he is going straight through. But now tell me about yourself," said Bonnie, affectionately passing an arm round Sylvia and making sure that she was well wrapped up. "Did you have a pleasant journey? Are you hungry? Or thirsty"

36

"Oh no, thank you. I had some provisions with me for the train. We had quite a pleasant journey. A wolf jumped into our compartment last night, but Mr. Grimshaw—that gentleman—stabbed it to death and we moved into another compartment."

"Is he a friend of yours?" Bonnie said, nodding over this incident.

"Oh dear no! I had never seen him before. Indeed, I did not like him *very* much," Sylvia confessed. "He seemed so strange, although I believe he meant to be kind."

The two children were silent for a moment or two, as the carriage galloped on its way. The soft rugs were delicious to Sylvia, and the grateful warmth of the foot warmer as it struck upward, gradually thawing her numbed and chilled feet, but the sweetest thing of all was the friendly pressure of Bonnie's hand and the loving brightness of her smile as she turned, every now and then, to scan her cousin.

"I can't believe you are really here at last!" she said. "I wonder which of us is the taller? What delightful times we shall have! Oh, I can't wait to show you everything—the ponies—my father has bought a new little quiet one for you, in case you are not used to riding—and the hothouse flowers, and my collections, and the wolfhounds. We shall have such games! And in the summer we can go for excursions on the wolds with the pony trap. If only Mamma and Papa did not have to go away it would be quite perfect."

She sighed.

"Poor Bonnie," said Sylvia impulsively, squeezing her cousin's hand. "Perhaps it will not have to be for very long." She received a grateful pressure in return, and they were silent again, listening to the crunch of the wheels on the snow and the cry of the wolf pack, now becoming fainter behind them in the distance.

There was something magical about this ride which Sylvia was to remember for the rest of her life—the dark, snow-scented air blowing constantly past them, the boundless wold and forest stretching away in all directions before and behind, the tramp and jingle of the horses, the snugness and security of the carriage, and above all Bonnie's happy welcoming presence beside her.

After a time Bonnie said, "I wonder how that poor man is. What did you say was his name?"

"Mr. Grimshaw."

Bonnie leaned across and plucked gently at his hand. "Mr. Grimshaw? Mr. Grimshaw? Are you any better?" But there was no reply. "He must be unconscious still," she said. "I wish we had some restoratives to give him—however, we shall be at home in another hour. Pattern and Mrs. Shubunkin will know what to do for him. Pattern is my maid—and oh! such a dear—and Mrs. Shubunkin is the housekeeper."

Presently Sylvia began to nod, and found her eyelids closing despite all her efforts to keep awake. But she had hardly more than dozed off when the carriage stopped with a clattering and a barking of dogs, and many shouts of greeting. Looking eagerly out of the window, she saw the great, rosy, glittering façade of Willoughby Chase, with every window shining a golden welcome. They had arrived.

Bonnie did not wait for James to open the carriage door. She had it unlatched in a moment and leaped out into the snow, turning to help her cousin with affectionate care. Sylvia was stiff and dazed with fatigue, and as Bonnie led her tenderly up the great curving flight of steps and into the hall she received only a vague impression of many lights and much warmth, people rushing hither and thither, and a kindly voice (that of Pattern, the maid) saying, "Poor little dear, she is wearied to death. James, do you carry her upstairs while I ask Mrs. Shubunkin for a posset."

The posset came, steaming, sweet, and delicious, and Pattern's gentle hands removed Sylvia's traveling clothes. Sylvia was too sleepy to study her surroundings before she

was placed between soft, smooth sheets and sank deep into dreamless slumber.

Later in the night she awoke, and saw stars shining beyond the white curtain at her bed's foot. Suddenly she recalled Aunt Jane's voice, teaching her astronomy: "There is Orion, Sylvia dear, and the constellation resembling a W is Cassiopeia." Oh, poor Aunt Jane! Would she be lying awake too, watching the stars? Would she be warm enough under the jet-trimmed mantle? What would she do at breakfast-time with no niece to warm the teapot, brew the Bohea, and make the toast gruel?

Tears began to run down Sylvia's cheeks and she drew a long breath, trying to suppress her silent sobs.

The next moment she heard feet patter across the carpet, and two small, comforting arms came round her neck. A cheek was rubbed lovingly against her wet one.

"What is it, Sylvia dear? Are you homesick? Shall I come into bed with you?"

Sylvia was on the point of revealing her worries about Aunt Jane. Then she realized that she must not. Aunt Jane's pride would not let her accept help from her brother, and so Sylvia must not disclose that she was lonely and cold and poor. But oh, somehow she must find a means of helping her aunt—she must! She must!

"Don't cry," Bonnie whispered. "This is your home now, and we shall do such delightful things together. I am sure I can make you happy." She hugged Sylvia again, and, slipping into the bed, began telling her of all the plans she had, for sledging and skating, and picking primroses in spring, and days on the moors in summer. Sylvia could not help being cheered by this happy prospect, and soon both children fell asleep, the dark head and the fair on one pillow.

Four

Next morning the children had breakfast together in the nursery, which was gay with the sunshine that sparkled on crystal and silver and found golden lights in the honey and quince preserve.

Miss Slighcarp, it seemed, was to take her meals in her own apartments, and of this Sylvia was glad, for when she met the governess after breakfast she found her a somewhat frightening lady, cold and severe and forbidding. However, Aunt Jane had taught Sylvia well, and in many respects it was found that she was ahead of Bonnie.

"You will have to work, miss," said Miss Slighcarp curtly to Bonnie. "You will have to work hard to catch up with your cousin."

"I am glad," said Bonnie, hugging Sylvia. "I want to work hard. It is delightful that you are so clever, we shall study all sorts of interesting things, botany and Greek and the use of the globes."

They did not do many lessons that morning. After they had lain on their backboards while Miss Slighcarp read them a short chapter of Egyptian history, they were dismissed to their own devices. Sir Willoughby and Lady Green would be departing at midday, and he wanted to instruct Miss Slighcarp in various matters relating to the running of the estate and household, of which she was to be in charge while he was away.

"Let us go and see how poor Mr. Grimshaw is this morning," Bonnie proposed. "I am longing to take you to Mamma and Papa, but Miss Slighcarp is with them now. We will wait until she comes back."

They ran along to the chamber where the unfortunate traveler had been placed, and found there an elderly whiskered gentleman, Dr. Morne, in consultation with round, rosy

Mrs. Shubunkin, the housekeeper. They curtsied to the doctor, who patted their heads absently.

"It is a most unusual case," he was saying to Mrs. Shubunkin. "The poor gentleman has recovered consciousness, but he has clean lost all recollection of his name and address and who he is. I have ordered him some medicines, and he must be kept very quiet and remain in bed until his memory returns. I will go and speak to Sir Willoughby on the matter."

"Perhaps if he were to see Sylvia he would remember the train journey," Bonnie suggested. "He told you his name, did he not, Sylvia?"

"Yes—Mr. Grimshaw, Josiah Grimshaw."

"It would be worth a trial," the doctor agreed, and, a footman just then arriving to inform him that Sir Willoughby was at liberty, he left them, while the children ventured unescorted into Mr. Grimshaw's chamber.

What was their surprise to discover that the patient was not in bed but up and standing by the fire, wrapped in a crimson plush dressing gown! Moreover, he seemed to have been burning papers, for the fireplace was full of black ash, and the room of blue smoke. He started violently as they entered, slammed shut the lid of a small dispatch box, and flung himself back into bed.

"What the deuce are you doing here?" he growled. "Who are you?"

"Don't you remember Sylvia, Mr. Grimshaw!" said Bonnie. "I am Bonnie Green, and Sylvia is my cousin who traveled with you on the train yesterday."

"Never seen her in my life before. And name's not Grimshaw," he snapped. "Don't know what it is, but not Grimshaw."

"He's wandering, poor fellow," whispered Bonnie. "He must have got out of bed in delirium. We had best send Mrs. Shubunkin to sit with him and see he does not do himself a mischief."

Mr. Grimshaw was plainly most displeased at their presence in his room, so they went off to tell the housekeeper that the invalid should not be left alone.

"Now come," said Bonnie then, taking her cousin's hand,

"Papa and Mamma must be free now, for I saw Miss Slighcarp downstairs as we crossed the stairhead."

When they reached Lady Green's sitting room, they found
the doctor there speaking with Sir Willoughby.

"And so you will let this poor man remain here so long
as he is in need of attention?" the doctor was saying. "That
is most kind of you, Sir Willoughby, and like your liberal-
ity."

"Eh, well," Sir Willoughby said, "couldn't turn the poor
fellow out into the snow, what? Plenty of room here. He
can remain till he gets his wits back—till we return, if need
be. Looking after him will give the servants something to
do while we are away. You'll come in and see him from
time to time, Morne?"

The doctor departed, promising careful attendance on the
stranger and wishing Lady Green a speedy return to health.

"Nothing like a sea voyage, dear lady, to bring roses back
to the cheeks."

"And so this is Sylvia," said Lady Green very kindly,
when the doctor had gone. "I hope that you and Bonnie
are going to be dear friends and look after one another
when we are away."

"Oh yes, Mamma!" Bonnie exclaimed. "I love her already.
We are going to be so happy together . . ."

Then her face fell and her bright color faded, for at that
moment Lady Green's maid entered the room with wraps
and a traveling mantle.

"Are you leaving *now*, Mamma? So soon?"

"It wants but five minutes to midday, my child," said
Lady Green as she wearily allowed herself to be swathed
in her cloak. Sylvia observed how thin her aunt's wrists were,
how languid her beautiful dark eyes.

Silently the children followed downstairs in the bustle of
departure. Servants darted here and there, mound upon

mound of boxes went out to the chaise, Sir Willoughby tenderly supported his wife to the hall door. There she enveloped Bonnie in a long and loving embrace, had a warm kiss, too, for Sylvia, and, pale as death, allowed herself to be lifted into the carriage. They saw her face at the window, with her eyes fixed yearningly on Bonnie.

"It won't be long, Mamma," Bonnie called. Her voice was strained and dry.

"Not long, my darling."

"Be good children," said Sir Willoughby hurriedly. "Mind what Miss Slighcarp tells you, now." He pressed a golden sovereign into each of their hands, and jumped quickly into the carriage after his wife. "Ready, James!"

The whip cracked, the mettlesome horses blew great clouds of steam into the frosty air, and they were off. The carriage whirled over the packed snow of the driveway, passed beyond a grove of leafless trees, and was lost to view.

Without a word, Bonnie turned on her heel and marched up the stairs and along the passages to the nursery. Sylvia followed, her heart swollen with compassion. She longed to say some comforting words, but could think of none.

"It may not be long, Bonnie," she ventured at length.

Bonnie sat at the table, her hands tightly clenched together. "I will not, I *will* not cry," she was saying to herself.

At Sylvia's anxious, loving, compassionate voice she took heart a little, and gave her cousin a smile. "After all," she thought, "I am lucky to have Papa and Mamma even if they have gone away; poor Sylvia has no one at all."

"Come," she said, jumping up, "the sun is shining. I will show you some of the grounds. Let us go skating."

"But Bonnie dear, I have no skates, and I do not know how."

"Oh, it is the easiest thing in the world, I will soon show you; and as for skates, Papa thought of that already, look . . ." Bonnie pulled open a cupboard door and showed six pairs of white kid skating boots, all different sizes. "We knew your feet must be somewhere near the same size as mine, since we are the same age, so Papa had several different pairs made and we thought one of them was certain to fit."

Sure enough, one of the pairs of boots fitted exactly. Sylvia was much struck by this thought on the part of her uncle, and astonished at the lavishness of having six pairs made for one to be chosen.

Likewise, Pattern pulled out a whole series of white fur caps and pelisses, and tried them against Sylvia until she found ones that fitted. "I've hung your green velvet in the closet, miss," she said. "Green velvet's all very well for London, but you want something warmer in the country."

Sylvia could not help a pang as she remembered the cutting of the green velvet shawl and saw the sumptuous pile of white fur; how she wished she might send one of the pelisses to Aunt Jane. But next moment Bonnie caught her hand and pulled her to the door.

"Don't go outside the park now, Miss Bonnie," Pattern said.

"We won't," Bonnie promised.

Snug in their furs, the two children ran out across the great snow-covered slope in front of the house, through the grove, and down to where a frozen river meandered across the park, after falling over two or three artificial cascades, now stiff and gleaming with icicles.

The children sat on a garden bench to put on their skates. Then, with much laughter and encouragement, Bonnie began to show Sylvia how to keep her balance on the ice.

"Why, Sylvia, you might have been born to it, you are a thousand times better than I was when I began."

"Perhaps it is because Aunt Jane took such pains teaching me to curtsy and dance the gavotte balancing Dr. Johnson's Dictionary on my head," Sylvia suggested, as she cautiously glided across to the opposite snow-piled bank and then hurriedly returned to the safety of Bonnie's helping hand.

"Whatever the reason, it is perfectly splendid! We can go right down the river to the end of the park, much farther skating than we can walking. The wolves, you see, cannot catch us on the ice."

"Is the river frozen all the way down?"

"Yes, all the way to the sea. Oh, I can't wait for you to see this countryside in summer," Bonnie said, as they skated carefully downstream. "The river is not nearly so full then, it is just a shallow, rocky stream, and we bathe, and paddle, and the banks are covered with heather and rockrose, it is so pretty."

"Is it far to the sea?"

"Oh, far—far. Fifty miles. First you come to Blastburn, which is a hideous town, all coal pits and ugly mills. Papa goes there sometimes on business. And then at the sea itself there is Rivermouth, where Papa and Mamma will go on board their ship the *Thessaly*." Bonnie sighed and skated a few yards in silence. "Why! she exclaimed suddenly, "is not that Miss Slighcarp over there? It is not very safe to go walking so near the park's boundary. The wolves have more than once been known to get in. I wonder if she knows, or if we should warn her?"

"Are you sure it is Miss Slighcarp?" said Sylvia, straining her eyes to study the gray figure walking beside a distant coppice.

"I think it is. Are you tired, Sylvia? Can you manage another half-mile? If we continue down the river it will curve round and bring us near to her. I think we should remind her about the wolves."

Sylvia protested that she was not at all tired, that she could easily skate for another hour, two hours if necessary, and, increasing their speed, the children hastened on down the frozen stream. The bank soon hid Miss Slighcarp from their sight.

"It is very imprudent of her," Bonnie commented. "I suppose, coming from London, she does not realize about the wolves."

Sylvia, secretly, began to be a little anxious. They seemed to have come a very long way, the house was nearly out of sight across the rolling parkland, and when they rounded the curve of the river they saw that Miss Slighcarp had cut across another ridge and was almost as far from them as ever. Sylvia's legs and back, unused to this form of exercise, began to feel tired and to ache, but she valiantly strove to keep up with the sturdier Bonnie.

"Just round this next bend," Bonnie encouraged her, "and then we *must* meet her. If not, I do not know what we can do—we shall have reached the park boundary, and moreover, the river runs into woods here, and the ice is treacherous and full of broken branches."

They passed the bend and saw a figure—but not the figure they expected. A stout woman in a red velvet jacket was walking away from them briskly into the wood. She was not Miss Slighcarp, nor in the least like her.

"It isn't she!" exclaimed Sylvia.

At the sound of her voice the woman swung round sharply and seemed to give them an angry look. Then she hurried on into the wood and disappeared. A moment later they heard the sound of horses' hoofs and the rumbling of carriage wheels.

"How peculiar! Can we have been mistaken? But no, we could not have confused a gray dress with a red one," Sylvia said.

Bonnie was frowning. "I do not understand it! What can a strange woman in a carriage have been doing in our woods? The road runs through there, but it goes nowhere save to the house."

"Perhaps when we get back we shall find her. Perhaps she is a neighbor come calling," Sylvia suggested.

Bonnie shook her head. "There are no neighbors." Then she seized Sylvia's arm. "Look! *There* is Miss Slighcarp!" Sure enough, the gray figure they had first observed was now to be seen, far away behind them, walking swiftly in the direction of the house.

"She must have turned back when we were between the high banks," Bonnie said repentantly. "And I have brought you so far! Poor Sylvia, I am afraid that you are dreadfully tired."

"Nonsense!" Sylvia said stoutly. "We had to come. And I shall manage very well."

But she was really well-nigh exhausted, and could not

help skating more and more slowly. Bonnie bit her lip and looked anxious. The sky was becoming overcast with the promise of more snow, and, worse, it would not be long until dusk.

"I have done very wrong," Bonnie said remorsefully. "I should have made you turn back, and come on myself."

"I should not have let you."

A sudden wind got up, and sent loose snow from the banks in a scurry across the gray ice. One or two large flakes fell from the sky.

"Can you go a little faster?" Bonnie could not conceal the anxiety in her tone. "Try, Sylvia!"

Sylvia exerted herself valiantly, but she was really so tired that she could hardly force her limbs to obey her.

"I am so stupid!" she said, half-laughing, half-crying. "Suppose I sit here on the bank, Bonnie, while you go home for assistance?"

Bonnie looked as if she were half-considering this proposal when a low moaning sound rose in the distance, a sound familiar to Bonnie, and, since yesterday, full of terrible significance for Sylvia. It was the far-off cry of wolves.

"No, that is not to be thought of," Bonnie said decisively. "I have a better plan. We must take off our skates. Can you manage? Make haste, then!"

They sat on a clump of rush by the river's edge, and with chilled fingers tugged at the knots in their bootlaces. Sylvia shivered as once again the wolf cry stole over the frozen parkland; it had been bad enough heard from the train, but *now*, when there was nothing between them and those pitiless legions, how dread it sounded!

The children stood up, slinging their skates round their necks.

"Now we must climb this little hill," Bonnie said. "Here, I'll take your hand. Can you run? Famous! Sylvia, you are

50

the bravest creature in the world, and when we get home I shall give you my little ivory workbox to show how sorry I am for having led you into such a scrape."

Sylvia did her best to smile at her cousin, having no breath to answer, and tried to stifle all doubts that they ever *would* get home.

Arrived at the top of the hill, Bonnie stood still and, as it seemed to Sylvia, wasted precious moments while she glanced keenly about her through the rapidly thickening snowstorm.

"Ah!" she cried presently. "The temple of Hermes! We must go this way." She tugged Sylvia at a run down the slope and across a wide intervening stretch of open ground toward a little pillared pavilion that stood on an artificial knoll against some dark trees. They had now put the river between them and the cry of the wolves, which was comforting, but Sylvia was dismayed to see that Bonnie was once more leading her away from the house.

"Where are we going, Bonnie?" she panted, fighting bravely to keep up.

"I have a friend who lives in the woods," Bonnie returned. "I only hope he is not away. Let us rest a moment here."

They stood struggling to get their breath in the temple of Hermes, which was no more than a roof supported on slender columns.

"Oh, Bonnie, look, look!" Sylvia cried in uncontrollable alarm, pointing back the way they had come. Through the dusk they could just distinguish two small black dots at the top of the slope, which were soon joined by several others. After a moment all these dots began coursing swiftly down the hillside in their direction.

"There is not a moment to be lost," Bonnie said urgently. "Make haste, make haste!" Half-leading, half-supporting the exhausted Sylvia, she urged her on through the deepening wood. Here Bonnie seemed to know her way almost by instinct. She passed from tree to tree, scanning them, apparently, for signs invisible to her cousin.

"Here we are!" she exclaimed in a tone of unutterable thankfulness, and, to Sylvia's astonishment, she put her fingers to her lips and gave vent to a long, clear whistle. More surprising still, she was instantly answered by another whistle which seemed to come from the very ground beneath their feet.

A clear, ringing voice called, "Here, Miss Bonnie! Here, quick!"

Sylvia found a lithe, bright-eyed boy beside her, helping her on. Taller than Bonnie, he was dressed entirely in skins. He wore a fur cap, carried a bow, and had a sheaf of arrows slung over his shoulder.

As the first of the wolf pack found their track in the temple of Hermes and came raging after, along the clear scent, the boy turned, fitted an arrow to his bow, and sent it unerringly into the midst of the pursuers. One wolf fell, and his companions immediately hurled themselves upon him with starving ferocity.

"That gives us a breathing space!" the boy exclaimed. "Inside, Miss Bonnie! Don't lose a moment."

With Bonnie tugging at her hand, and the boy guarding the rear, threatening the wolves with his bow, Sylvia found herself whisked down a long narrow path, or passageway, snow-lined at first, then floored with dead leaves. It was dark, she was in a cave! And more curious still, she could feel a number of live creatures pushing against her legs, almost overbalancing her. They were soft and smooth, and she could hear an angry hissing coming from them which almost drowned the clamor of the wolves outside. She would have cried out in fright if she had had any breath left—and then she and Bonnie rounded a corner in the passage and saw before them the comfortable glow of a fire burning on a sandy hearth.

Heaped-up piles of ferns and dead leaves, covered with furs, lay against the cave walls, and on these Bonnie and Sylvia flung themselves, for even Bonnie could now acknowledge that she was nearly fainting from weariness.

"There!" said the boy, following them in. "I've shut the gate. They'll not catch you this time! But what was you doing, Miss Bonnie, so far from the house on a night like this? It's not like you to take such a foolish risk."

As Bonnie began explaining how it had come about, Sylvia was amazed to see a number of large white geese waddle after the boy into the cave. They looked rather threateningly out of their flat, black, beady eyes at Sylvia and Bonnie. One or two of them thrust out their necks and hissed, but the boy waved them back into the passage and flung them a handful of corn to keep them quiet.

Lulled by the flickering firelight and the long white necks weaving up and down in the entrance as the geese pecked their corn, Sylvia, who was half-stupefied by exhaustion, fell fast asleep.

When she awoke it was to the sound of voices. Bonnie was saying anxiously:

"But Simon, we cannot stay here all night! My dear Pattern will be so worried! She will be certain the wolves have got us. And Miss Slighcarp, too, will be concerned. Perhaps they have already sent the men out searching for us."

"I'll have a look in a moment," the boy returned. "Now, if you'll wake your cousin, miss, the cakes are ready, and you'll both feel better on full stomachs than empty."

He spoke with a pleasant country burr. Sylvia, lying drowsy on her heap of leaves, thought that his voice had a comfortable, brown, furry sound to it.

"Sylvia! Wake up!" Bonnie said. "Here's Simon made us

53

some delicious cakes. And if you are like me you are ravenous with hunger."

"Indeed I am!" Rubbing her eyes and smiling, Sylvia brushed off the leaves and sat up.

The boy had separated the fire into two glowing hillocks. From between these he now pulled a flat stone on which were baking a number of little cakes. The two children ate them hungrily as soon as they were cool enough to hold. They were brown on the outside, white and floury within, and sweet to the taste.

"Your cakes are splendid, Simon," Bonnie said. "How do you make them?"

"From chestnut flour, Miss Bonnie. I gather up the chestnuts in the autumn and pound them to flour between two stones."

While they were eating he went along the entrance passage. In a minute he came back to say, "Wolves have gone, and it's a fine, sharp night, all spiky with stars. No signs of men out searching, Miss Bonnie. It's my belief we'd best be off now while the way's clear. Do you think you can walk as far as the house now, Miss Sylvia?"

"Oh yes, yes! I feel perfectly rested," declared Sylvia. But she was obliged to acknowledge when she stood up that she still found herself stiff and tired, and would be unable to keep up a very fast pace.

"I have badly overtaxed your strength this first day," exclaimed Bonnie self-reproachfully. "Still, if you *can* walk, Sylvia, I think we should be off now and save our poor Pattern some hours of dreadful worry."

"Certainly I can walk," Sylvia said stoutly, "let us start at once," though inwardly her heart quailed somewhat at the thought of the wolves very likely still in the neighborhood.

"A moment before we start." The boy Simon dug in shallow sand at the side of the cave and brought out a large leather bottle and a horn drinking cup. He gave the girls each a small drink from the bottle. It was strong, heady stuff, tasting of honey.

"That will hearten you for the walk," he said.

"What is it, Simon?"

"Metheglin, miss. I make it in the summer from the heather honey."

He picked up his bow and flung a few logs on the fire. The children resumed their furs, which they had taken off at their first entry into the warm cave.

"I do love your home, Simon!" Bonnie exclaimed. "I hate to leave it!"

"*You*, miss?" he said, grinning, "with your grand house and a different room for each day in the year?"

"Well, yes, of course I love that too, but this is so snug!"

Simon quieted the geese, who raised their necks and hissed as the children passed them.

"I wish I had another weapon to defend you with," he muttered. "One bow is hardly sufficient for three. I will cut you a cudgel when we are outside, Miss Bonnie."

"I know, Simon!" Bonnie cried. "My old fowling piece that I left here that rainy day last autumn! I have never thought of it since. Have you it still?"

"Of course I have," he said, his face lighting up. "And carefully oiled, too, with neat's-foot oil. It is in good order, Miss Bonnie. I am glad you reminded me of it—what a fool I was not to think of it before!"

He took it down from where it hung on the passage wall in a leather sack. Bonnie, somewhat to her cousin's alarm and amazement, handled the gun confidently and soon satisfied herself of its being in excellent order and ready to fire.

"Now let us be off," she said gaily. "I can keep the villains at a distance with this."

They went out into the clear, sparkling night. The new snow, which had obliterated both their footprints and those of the wolves, made a crisp carpet beneath their feet. Bonnie and Simon kept a vigilant lookout for wolves, and Sylvia did too, though secretly she felt she was almost less afraid of the wolves than of her cousin Bonnie's gun. However, there was no occasion to use the fowling piece, as the wolves appeared to have left that region for the moment, drawn away, doubtless, by some new quarry.

Their journey back to the house was quiet and uninterrupted.

"It is strange," remarked Bonnie in a puzzled voice, "that we do not see men out everywhere with lanterns searching for us. Why, the time I was late back from picking wild strawberries, my father had every man on the estate out with pitchforks and muskets!"

"Aye," said Simon, "but your father's from home now, isn't he, Miss Bonnie?"

"Yes he is," answered Bonnie sighing. "I suppose that is the reason."

And she fell into rather a sad silence.

When they reached the great terrace, Bonnie suggested that they should go in by a side entrance, and thus avoid informing Miss Slighcarp of their return.

"For it is possible that Pattern, fearing her anger, has left her in ignorance that we were out," she suggested thoughtfully. "I believe Pattern is a little frightened of Miss Slighcarp."

"I am sure *I* am," Sylvia agreed. "There is something so cold and glittering about her eyes, and then her voice is so disagreeable. I dare say that is the reason, Bonnie."

As they passed a large, lighted window, Bonnie murmured, "That is the great library, Sylvia, where my father keeps all his books and papers. I will show you over it tomorrow . . . Why, what a curious thing!" she exclaimed. For, glancing in as they walked by, they saw Miss Slighcarp, under the illumination of numerous candles, apparently hard at work searching through a mass of papers. There were papers on chairs, on tables, on the floor. Beyond her, at the far end of the room, similarly engaged, was a gentleman who looked amazingly like Mr. Grimshaw. Could it be he? But at the slight noise made by their feet on the snow, Miss Slighcarp turned. She could not see the watchers, who were beyond the lighted area near the window, but she crossed with a decisive step and flung-to the heavy velvet curtains shutting off the scene within.

"What can she be doing?" Bonnie exclaimed. "And was not that Mr. Grimshaw? Dr. Morne said he should not get out of bed!"

"Perhaps she is familiarizing herself with the contents of

your father's papers," Sylvia suggested. "Did you not say she was to look after the estate? And I am not *sure* that was Mr. Grimshaw. We had hardly time to see."

Arrived at the little postern door, they had scarcely knocked before it was flung open and Pattern had enveloped them in her arms.

"Oh, you naughty, naughty, precious children! How could you? How *could* you? Here's my poor heart been nearly broke in half with fright at thinking you was eaten by the wolves, and Miss Slighcarp saying no such thing, you'd come home soon, and me saying 'Begging your pardon, miss, but you don't know this park and these wolves as I do,' and begging, *begging* her to tell the men and sound the alarm, but no, my lady knows best what's to be done and it's my belief nothing ever *would* have been done till we found some boots and buttons of you in the snow and the rest all ate up by wolves if you hadn't come home all by yourselves, you good, wicked, precious, naughty lambs—*oh!*" and the faithful Pattern relieved herself by a burst of tears.

"Not by ourselves, Pattern," said Bonnie, hugging her tightly. "Simon brought us home. We *were* chased by wolves —though it wasn't exactly our fault—and he hid us in his cave till they were gone."

"Never will I hear a word said against that boy. Some say he's a wicked, vagabond gypsy, but I saw he's the best-hearted, trustiest . . . Ask him in, Miss Bonnie, and I'll give him the Christmas pudding that was too big to go in my lady's valise."

But the silent Simon, overwhelmed, perhaps, by Pattern's flow of words, had melted away into the night without waiting to be thanked.

"Will he be all right?" breathed Sylvia, big-eyed with horror. "Won't the wolves get him on the way home?"

"I don't believe they could ever catch him," Bonnie re-assured her. "He can run so fast! Besides he has his bow, and then, too, he can climb trees and swing from branch to branch if they get near him."

"Never mind about him, nothing ever hurts Simon," bustled Pattern, half-pushing, half-pulling them up the lit-tle back stairs. "Come on with you now till I get a posset inside you."

Cold in spite of their furs, the children were glad to be sat down before a glowing fire in the night nursery, while Pattern scolded and clucked, and brushed the tangles out of their hair, brought in with her own hands the big silver bathtub filled with steaming water, in which bunches of lemon mint had been steeped, giving a deliciously fragrant scent, and bathed them each in turn, afterward wrapping them in voluminous warm white flannel gowns.

Next she fetched little pipkins of hot, savory soup, sternly saw every mouthful swallowed, and finally hustled them both into Bonnie's big, comfortable bed with the blue swans flying on its curtains.

"For if there's any nightmares about wolves, at least that way you'll be able to comfort each other," she muttered. "And as for Miss Slighcarp, let *her* rest in uncertainty till the morning, for I'm not going to her again. Coming home soon, indeed! As if such a thing were likely!"

And off she tiptoed, leaving a rose-scented nightlight burning and the peaceful crackle of the fire to lull them to sleep.

Five

The next morning dawned gray and lowering. Snow was falling fast out of the heavy sky, the flakes hurrying down like dirty feathers from a leaking mattress. Pattern let the children sleep late, and though when they woke she cosseted them by giving them breakfast in front of the nursery fire, it was not a happy meal. Sylvia felt stiff and tired from her unusual exertions the day before, while poor Bonnie was thinking every minute of her parents' absence: wondering how they had fared on their journey so far, noticing the sad, unaccustomed quietness of the house, which was generally filled with bustle—servants running to and fro, stamp of horses, and her father shouting his orders because he was too impatient to ring the bell.

Sylvia kindly tried to distract her by asking questions about Simon, the boy in the woods.

"Has he always lived in that cave, Bonnie? It seems so strange! Has he no father or mother?"

Bonnie shook her head. "None that he knows of. He came to my father four or five years ago, one autumn day, and asked if he might live in that cave in the park; he said that he had been working for a farmer but the man ill-treated him and he had walked half across England to get away from him. My father asked what he proposed to live on. He said, chestnuts and goose eggs. He had a goose and a gander that he had reared from chicks. Papa took a fancy to him and told him that he might try it—there are hundreds of chestnut trees in the park—but he said Simon wasn't to come whining to him if he got hungry, he'd have to turn to and work for his living as a garden boy."

"And did he?"

"Work as a garden boy? No, he lived on chestnuts and reared a great many geese. Mrs. Shubunkin buys eggs from him, and every spring Simon drives his geese up to London and sells them at the Easter Fair. He gets on famously. Father often says he wishes he had as few worries." Bonnie sighed.

"I wonder if he will always continue to live in the cave," Sylvia was beginning, when Pattern came in to clear away the breakfast things.

"Now then, Miss Bonnie and Miss Sylvia, nearly lesson time, my dearies, so make haste and get dressed." They had been breakfasting in warm wadded satin dressing gowns.

"This is not my frock, Pattern," said Sylvia, looking admiringly at the clothes the maid had brought her. There was a soft, thick woolen dress in a beautiful deep shade of blue that exactly matched her eyes. "It is a great deal prettier than anything of mine."

"It's one I ran up for you yesterday, Miss Sylvia," Pattern said kindly. "My Lady Green, bless her good heart, thought you might be needing some warmer dresses for the country, but didn't like to have anything made for you until she knew what colors suited you best. Before she left yesterday she bade me make up one out of this cloth, which she had ready with a number of others. There!" she added, fastening Sylvia's dress at the back and turning her round. "If that doesn't bring out the color of your eyes! And here's some ribbons to match for your hair."

Sylvia's eyes none the less filled with tears at the thought that her aunt, so ill and grief-stricken at the idea of parting from her home, could still spare time for such thoughtfulness.

"Come along," said Bonnie, who meanwhile had been hurriedly putting on a dark-red cashmere with a white lace collar, "we shall be late for our lessons."

The two children ran to the schoolroom while Pattern carefully folded and put away Sylvia's white dress.

Miss Slighcarp had not yet arrived, and the children beguiled the time by wandering round the room and looking at the many beautiful pictures that hung on its walls; then, as the governess still did not appear, Bonnie took Sylvia through a door leading out of the schoolroom into her toyroom.

This was a large and beautiful apartment, carpeted in blue, its wall white, its ceiling all a-sparkle with gilt stars. In it was every imaginable toy, and many that Sylvia never had imagined even in her most wistful dreams. Occupying the place of honor in the middle of the floor was a stately rocking horse covered with real gray horsehair, and so cunningly carved that he seemed alive. His crystal eyes shone with intelligence.

"That's 'Dolphus," said Bonnie, giving him a careless hug as she passed. "Then those are all the dolls, in that row of little chairs. The largest is Miranda, the smallest, at this end (she's my favorite) is Conchita."

Sylvia's hand curled lovingly round Annabelle, hidden in her pocket, but she resolved not to introduce her to this galaxy of beauties until the kind Pattern had accomplished her promise and made a new dress for her from a leftover piece of the blue material. Then, Sylvia thought, Annabelle would be quite presentable, and some of the smaller dolls did not look at all proud.

"This is the dolls' house," Bonnie said. "Grown-ups aren't allowed inside, but you can come in, of course, Sylvia, whenever you like."

The dolls' house, large enough to get into, was a cottage with real thatch (and real canaries nesting in it). There was a balcony, stairs, two stories, a cooking stove that really worked, and a lot of genuine Queen Anne furniture, including a beautiful walnut chest full of Queen Anne clothes that fitted the children.

Sylvia was trying a blue velvet cloak against her, and Bonnie was saying, "Come and look at the other toys, you haven't seen half yet . . ." when they were interrupted by a cough from the schoolroom and hurriedly bundled the clothes back into the chest.

"I'll show you the rest this afternoon," whispered Bonnie, waving her hand toward a large cupboard in the wall with double glass doors. Sylvia had a tantalizing glimpse of numerous variously shaped brightly colored toys on its shelves as they ran back into the schoolroom.

"I'm so sorry we were not in the room to welcome you, Miss Slighcarp," Bonnie began in her impulsive way, and then she stopped abruptly. Sylvia noticed her turn extremely pale.

The governess, who had been examining some books on the shelves, swung round with equal abruptness. She seemed astonished to see them.

"Where have you been?" she demanded angrily, after an instant's pause.

"Why," Sylvia faltered, "merely in the next room, Miss Slighcarp."

But Bonnie, with choking utterance, demanded, "Why are you wearing my mother's dress?"

Sylvia had observed that Miss Slighcarp had on a draped

64

gown of old gold velvet with ruby buttons, far grander than the gray twill she had worn the day before.

"Don't speak to me in that way, miss!" retorted Miss Slighcarp in a rage. "You have been spoiled all your life,

but we shall soon see who is going to be mistress now. Go to your place and sit down. Do not speak until you are spoken to."

Bonnie paid not the slightest attention. "Who said you could wear my mother's best gown?" she repeated. Sylvia, alarmed, had slipped into her place at the table, but Bonnie, reckless with indignation, stood in front of the governess, glaring at her.

"Everything in this house was left entirely to my personal disposition," Miss Slighcarp said coldly.

"But not her clothes! Not to wear! How *dare* you? Take it off at once! It's no better than stealing!"

Two white dents had appeared on either side of Miss Slighcarp's nostrils.

"Another word and it's the dark cupboard and bread-and-water for you, miss," she said fiercely.

"I don't care what you say!" Bonnie stamped her foot. "Take off my mother's dress!"

Miss Slighcarp boxed Bonnie's ears, Bonnie seized Miss Slighcarp's wrists. In the confusion a bottle of ink was knocked off the table, spilling a long blue trail down the gold velvet skirt. Miss Slighcarp uttered an exclamation of fury.

"Insolent, ungovernable child! You shall suffer for this!" With iron strength she thrust Bonnie into a closet containing crayons, globes, and exercise books, and turned the key on her. Then she swept from the room.

Sylvia remained seated, aghast, for half a second. Then she ran to the cupboard door—but alas! Miss Slighcarp had taken the key with her.

"Bonnie! Bonnie! Are you all right? It's I, Sylvia."

She could hear bitter sobs.

"Don't cry, Bonnie, please don't cry. I'll run after her and beg her to let you out. I dare say she will, once she has reflected. She can't have known it was your mother's *favorite* gown."

Bonnie seemed not to have heard her. "Mamma, Mamma!" Sylvia could hear her sobbing. "Oh, why did you have to go away?"

How Sylvia longed to be able to batter down the cupboard door and get her arms round poor Bonnie! But the door was thick and massive, with a strong lock, quite beyond her power to move. Since she could not attract Bonnie's attention, she ran after Miss Slighcarp.

After vainly knocking at the governess's bedroom door she went in without waiting for a summons (a deed of exceptional bravery for the timid Sylvia). Nobody was there. The ink-stained velvet dress lay flung carelessly on the floor, crushed and torn, so great had Miss Slighcarp's haste been to remove it.

Sylvia hurried out again and began to search through the huge house, wandering up this passage and down that, through galleries, into golden drawing rooms, satin-hung boudoirs, billiard rooms, ballrooms, croquet rooms. At last she found the governess in the Great Hall, surrounded by servants.

Miss Slighcarp did not see Sylvia. She had changed into what was very plainly another of Lady Green's gowns, a rose-colored crêpe with aiguillettes of diamonds on the shoulders. It did not fit her very exactly.

She seemed to be giving the servants their wages. Sylvia wondered why many of the maids were crying, and why the men looked in general angry and rebellious, until she realized that Miss Slighcarp was paying them off and dismissing them. When the last one had been given his little packet of money, she announced:

"Now, let but a glimpse of your faces be seen within ten miles of this house, and I shall send for the constables!"

Then she added to a man who stood beside her, "Ridiculous, quite ridiculous, to keep such a large establishment of idle good-for-nothings, kicking their heels, eating their heads off."

"Just so, ma'am, just so," he assented. Sylvia was amazed to recognize Mr. Grimshaw, apparently quite restored to health, and in full possession of his faculties. He held a small blunderbuss, and was waving it threateningly, to urge the departing servants out of the great doors and on their way into the snowstorm.

"What a strange thing!" thought Sylvia in astonishment. "Can he be recovered? Or was he never really ill? Can he have known Miss Slighcarp before? He seemed so different on the train."

At that moment she heard a familiar voice beside her, in the rapidly thinning crowd of servants, and found Pattern at her elbow.

"Miss Sylvia, dear! Thank the good Lord I saw you. That wicked Jezebel is paying us all off and sending us away, but she needn't think *I'm* going to go and leave my darling Miss Bonnie. Do you and she come along to the little blue powder room, Miss Sylvia, this afternoon at five, and we'll talk over what's best to be done."

"But Bonnie can't! She's locked up!" gasped Sylvia. "In the schoolroom cupboard!"

"She never has . . . ! *Oh*, what wouldn't I give to get my hands round that she-devil's throat," muttered Pattern. "That's because she knew Miss Bonnie would never stand tamely by and let her father's old servants be packed off into the snow. Let her out, Miss Sylvia! Let her out of it quick! She never could endure to be shut up."

"But I can't! Miss Slighcarp has the key."

"There's another—in the little mother-of-pearl cabinet in the anteroom where the javelins hang."

Sylvia did not wait. She remembered how to find her way to the little anteroom, and she flew on winged feet to the mother-of-pearl cabinet. She found the key, ran to the schoolroom, opened the door, and in no time had her cheek pressed lovingly against Bonnie's tear-stained one.

"Oh, you poor precious! Oh, Bonnie, she's wicked, Miss Slighcarp's really wicked! She's dismissing all the servants."

"What?" Bonnie was distracted from her own grief and indignation by the tale Sylvia poured out.

"Let us go at once," she exclaimed, "at *once,* and stop it!" But when they passed the big schoolroom window they saw the lonely procession of servants, far away, toiling across a snow-covered ridge in the park.

"We are too late," said Sylvia in despair. Bonnie gazed after the tiny, distant figures, biting her lips.

"Is Pattern gone too?" she asked, turning to Sylvia.

"I believe not. I believe she means to hide somewhere about the house." Sylvia told Bonnie of Pattern's wish to meet them that afternoon.

"Oh, she is good! She is faithful!" exclaimed Bonnie.

"But will it not be very dangerous for her?" Sylvia said doubtfully. "Miss Slighcarp threatened to send for the constables if she saw any of the servants near the house. She might have Pattern sent to prison!"

"I do not believe Pattern would let herself be caught. There are so many secret hiding places about the house. And in any case all the officers are our friends round here."

At that moment the children were startled by the sound of approaching voices. One of them was Miss Slighcarp's. Sylvia turned pale.

"She must not find you out of the cupboard. Hide, quickly, Bonnie!"

She relocked the cupboard door, and pocketed the key. As there was no time to lose, the two children slipped be-

69

hind the window curtain. Miss Slighcarp entered with the footman, James.

"As I have done you the favor of keeping you on when all the others were dismissed, sirrah," she was saying, "you will have to work for your wages as never before."

The blue velvet curtains behind which the children stood were pounced all over with tiny crystal disks, encircled with seed pearls. The little disks formed miniature windows, and, setting her eye to one, Bonnie could see that James's good-natured face wore a sullen expression, which he was attempting to twist into an evil leer.

"First, you must take out and crate all these toys. Put them into packing cases. They are to be sent away and sold. It is quite ridiculous to keep this amount of gaudy rubbish for the amusement of two children."

"Yes, ma'am."

"At dinnertime bring some bread-and-water on a tray for Miss Green, who is locked up in that cupboard."

"Shall I let her out, ma'am?"

"Certainly not. She is a badly behaved, ill-conditioned child, and must be disciplined. She may be let out this evening at half-past eight. Here is the key."

"Yes, ma'am."

"The other child, Miss Sylvia Green, may lunch in the schoolroom as usual. Plain food, mind. Nothing fancy. From now on the children are to make their own beds, sweep their own rooms, and wash their own plates and clothes."

"Yes, ma'am."

"After dinner I wish you to see to the grooming of the horses and ponies. They are all to be sold save four carriage horses."

"The children's ponies as well, ma'am?"

"Certainly! I shall find more suitable occupations for the children than such idle and extravagant pursuits! Now I am going to be busy in the Estate Room. You may bring me a light luncheon at one o'clock: chicken, oyster patties, trifle, and a half-bottle of champagne."

She swept out of the room. The moment she had gone James went quickly to the closet and unlocked it, saying in a low voice, "She's gone now, Miss Bonnie, you can come out."

He seemed greatly astonished to find the cupboard empty, but next minute the children ran out from behind the curtain.

"James, James!" cried Bonnie, "what does it all mean? How dare she sell my toys, and Papa's horses? What is she doing it for?"

"Why, she's wicked!" Sylvia exclaimed indignantly. "She's a fiend!"

"You're right, miss, she's a thorough wrong 'un," said James gloomily, when he had got over the surprise of Bonnie's not being in the cupboard after all. "How your pa came to be so deceived in her I'll never know."

"But he had never met her! It was arranged that she should come here to look after us by his lawyer in London, Mr. Gripe. And after all, she is a relative."

"Ah, I see," said James, scratching his head. "Even so, it's a puzzle to me why Sir Willoughby didn't rumble her when he saw her. One look at her face would be enough to show the sort she is, you'd think. But I suppose he was worried over her ladyship."

"But James, why is she dismissing the servants, and why has she kept you on?"

"Why, miss, I suppose she means to make hay while the sun shines—save the servants' wages and pop as much of your pa's money into her own pocket as she can while he's away. Then before he comes back, I suppose she'll be off. She's kept on three or four servants, just to look after her, like. The worst of it is, she's kept on all the untrustworthy ones, Groach, the keeper, and Marl, the steward that Sir Willoughby was giving another chance to after he was caught pilfering, and Prout, the undergroom that drinks—I dare say she liked the looks of their knavish faces. I saw how it was going, so I tried to make myself look as hangdog and sullen as I could, and the trick worked: she kept me on too. I couldn't abear to think of you, Miss Bonnie, and Miss Sylvia, being left all alone in the house with that harpy and such a pack of thieves. Poor Pattern had to go; in a mighty taking she was."

"But she hasn't gone far," Bonnie told him, and explained about the scheme to meet in the little blue powder room. James's face broke into a slow grin.

"I might ha' known she wouldn't be driven off so easily," he said. "Well, we'll have a proper old council then and decide what to do. In the meantime I'd better be getting on with packing up these things, Miss Bonnie, or I shall lose my place and not be able to help you."

"Pack up my toys? But you *can't!*" exclaimed Bonnie in grief and horror, looking at her treasured things. "Couldn't you hide them away in one of the attics?"

"Can't be, Miss Bonnie dear. She's going to go through 'em when they're in the boxes. I could save out a few, though, I dare say," James said pityingly.

Half-distracted, Bonnie looked among her toys, trying to decide which she could bear to part with—'Dolphus must go, for he would be missed, and so must the dolls' house and the bigger dolls, but she saved Conchita, her favorite, and an ivory paint box as big as a tea tray, and the skates, and some of the beautiful clothes from the dolls' house, while Sylvia mournfully sorted out the most interesting-looking and beautifully illustrated books from a large bookcase.

"Oh, and I must keep my little writing desk, James, for I mean to write to Papa this very day and tell him how wicked Miss Slighcarp is. Then he'll soon come home."

"I'll put the desk in the attic for you, miss," promised James, "but it's no use writing to your papa. Rather write to Mr. Gripe."

"Why, James?"

"Why, your papa's at sea now. His ship won't reach a port for three months."

"Oh dear—nor it will," said Bonnie sadly. "And I don't know Mr. Gripe's address in London. What shall I do? For we can't, *can't* endure this dreadfulness for three months— and then it would be another three months before Papa could come home, even supposing Mamma was well again."

Just then they heard Miss Slighcarp's step approaching once more, and her voice calling, "James, come here. I need your help to move a heavy deed box."

"I must go, miss," whispered James hurriedly. "Don't let yourself be seen. I'll bring your luncheon up by and by."

He hastened from the room.

The day passed unhappily. As Bonnie was supposed to be shut in the cupboard, she could not leave the schoolroom for fear of meeting Miss Slighcarp, and Sylvia would go nowhere without her. They tried various occupations, reading, sewing, drawing, but had not the heart to pursue them for long. At noon they heard Miss Slighcarp's voice in the passage outside. Bonnie whisked behind the curtain, but the governess did not come in. She was speaking to James again.

"Is that the young ladies' luncheon?"

"This is the bread-and-water for Miss Green, ma'am," he answered respectfully. "I'll fetch Miss Sylvia's tray when I've taken this in."

"She's not to come out of the cupboard to eat it, mind."

73

"No, ma'am."

He appeared, grinning broadly, planked a dry-looking loaf and a jug of water on the table, and then whispered, "Don't touch it, Miss Bonnie. Just as soon as the old cat's out of the way I'll bring something better!" And, sure enough, ten minutes later, he returned carrying a tray covered with a cloth which, when taken off, revealed two dear little roast partridges with bread sauce, red currant jelly, and vegetables.

"You'll not starve while I'm here to see after you," he whispered.

The children ate hungrily, and later James came back with a dish of trifle and took away the meat dishes, carefully covering them again with the cloth before venturing into the corridor.

"I wish I knew where the secret passage came out," he murmured. "Porson, the old steward, always used to say there was a sliding panel in this room and a passage that led down to the dairy. With that she-dragon on the prowl it would be rare and useful to have a secret way into here. You might have a bit of a search for it, Miss Bonnie."

"We'll begin at once!" exclaimed Bonnie. "It will be something to pass the time."

The moment James had taken away the pudding plates they began testing the walls for hidden springs.

"You start by the door, Sylvia, and I'll begin at the fireplace, and we'll each do two sides of the room," Bonnie suggested.

It was a big room, its walls covered in white linenfold paneling, decorated with carved garlands of roses painted blue. The children carefully pushed, pulled, and pressed each wooden rose, without result. An hour, two hours went by, and they were becoming disheartened and beginning to

74

feel that the story of the secret passage must have been merely an idle tale, when Sylvia suggested:

"We haven't tried the fireplace, Bonnie. Do you suppose it possible that part of the mantelpiece should be false?"

"Clever girl!" said Bonnie, giving her a hug. "Let us try it at once."

The mantel was large, and beautifully carved from some foreign stone and a gray, satiny surface. It extended for several feet on either side of the fireplace to form two wide panels on which were carved deer with elaborately branching antlers. The children ran to these and began fingering the antlers and trying to move them. Suddenly Sylvia gave an exclamation—as she pushed the deer's head to one side the whole panel slid away into the wall, leaving a dark aperture like a low, narrow doorway.

"You've found it!" breathed Bonnie. "Oh, what fun this is! Let us go in at once and see where it leads. Sylvia, you are the cleverest creature in the world, and I do not know what I should have done if you had not been here to keep me company. I could not have borne it!"

She was about to dart into the hole when the more prudent Sylvia said, "Should we not take lighted candles? I have heard that the air in this kind of disused passage is sometimes very foul and will put out a flame. If we had candles we should be warned in time."

"Very true! I did not think." Bonnie ran to a cupboard which held wax tapers in long silver holders and brought two each, which they kindled at the fire. Then they slipped cautiously through the narrow opening, Bonnie leading the way.

"We had better shut the panel behind us," she said. "Only imagine if Miss Slighcarp should come into the schoolroom and find it open!"

"What if we cannot open it again from the inside?"

"Perhaps it will be possible to leave just a crack."

Unfortunately the panel proved to be on some sort of spring. As soon as Sylvia touched it, it rolled smoothly shut. A small plaster knob seemed intended to open it from the inside, but when Bonnie rather impatiently pressed this, it crumbled away in her hand.

"How vexatious!" she said.

Sylvia was alarmed at the thought that they might have immured themselves for life, but Bonnie whispered stoutly:

"Never mind! The passage must come out somewhere, and if we are shut up, at least it is no worse than being shut up by Miss Slighcarp."

They tiptoed along, through thick, shuffling dust.

The passage was exceedingly narrow, and presently led them down a flight of steep steps. It was not pitch dark; here and there a tiny hole let in a glimmer of daylight, and, placing her eye to these holes, Bonnie was able to discover their whereabouts.

"Now we are behind the Great Hall, I can see the coats of arms. This is the silver-gilt anteroom. Now we are looking into the armory, those are gun-barrels. Imagine this passage having been here all this time and my never knowing of it! Oh, how I wish Papa and Mamma were at home! What famous times we should have, jumping out and surprising them! And we should discover a whole lot of secrets by overhearing people's private conversations."

"Would that be honorable?" Sylvia doubtfully whispered.

"Perhaps not with Papa and Mamma, but it would be quite another matter with Miss Slighcarp. I mean to listen to *her* all I can!"

They soon had an opportunity to do so, for the next peep-hole looked into the library, and when Bonnie put her eye to it she saw the governess in close consultation with Mr. Grimshaw. They were at the far end of the large room, and

76

at first out of earshot, but they soon moved nearer to the unseen watchers.

"Poke up the fire, Josiah," said Miss Slighcarp, who was studying a large parchment. "This must be burned at once, now that we have succeeded in finding it." The children heard Mr. Grimshaw stirring up the logs, and realizing that they must be standing beside the fireplace and that their spyhole was probably concealed in the chimneypiece. It was possible that there was another opening panel, similar to that in the schoolroom, but they were careful not to try pressing any projections, having no wish to be brought suddenly face to face with their enemies.

"Take the bellows and blow it into a blaze," Miss Slighcarp said. She was reading the document carefully. "What a good thing Sir Willoughby was careless enough to leave his will at home instead of keeping it with Mr. Gripe. It has saved us a deal of trouble."

"Indeed, yes," said Mr. Grimshaw comfortably. "And is it as you thought—does he leave everything to the child?"

"Almost everything," said Miss Slighcarp. She read on with compressed lips. "There is a legacy of twenty thousand pounds a year to his niece, a few hundred to me in gratitude for my services—pah!—and some trifling bequests to servants. Mention, too, of his sister Jane, my distant cousin. Is she likely to come poking her nose and being troublesome?"

"Not a fear of it," Mr. Grimshaw answered. "I made inquiries about her when I was in London. She is extremely elderly and unworldly; moreover, she is frail and unlikely to last long. She will never interfere with our management of the estate."

"Excellent. I will burn this will then—there, on the fire it goes—and you must set to work at once to forge another, leaving *everything* to me. Have you practiced the signature sufficiently?"

"I could do it with my left hand," Mr. Grimshaw said. "I have copied it from every document in this room." He drew a chair to a table at a little distance, pulled a piece of parchment toward him, and began slowly and carefully writing on it.

Miss Slighcarp, meanwhile, was tearing up and burning a great many other documents. "The more confusion his affairs are found to be in, the better," she observed. "It will give us the more time to make our plans."

"You sound very certain that he—that *the event* will take place. Suppose he should, after all, return?"

"My dear Josiah," said Miss Slighcarp meaningfully, "the master to whom I spoke was very certain about the state of the vessel. He said she could not last another voyage. But even if that plan should miscarry, what then? Sir W. cannot be back before a year is up. We shall have ample warning of his return and can be clear away and embarked for the colonies before he arrives. We shall never be caught."

"What of the children? You will not keep them here?"

"Not for long. They can go to Gertrude," said Miss Slighcarp ominously. "She will soon knock the nonsense out of them. Now, do not disturb me. I must master the details of this deed." She picked up another document and began studying it absorbedly.

The children tiptoed on.

"Bonnie," said Sylvia rather fearfully after a few moments, when she judged that they were well out of earshot of the library and its inmates, "what did Miss Slighcarp mean when she referred to the *event?* And why was she burning my uncle's will?"

"I am not certain," confessed Bonnie, who was pale and frowning over this new evidence of Miss Slighcarp's knavery, "but it is plain that she means nothing but wickedness."

Sylvia glanced in a troubled way at her cousin. It was

evident that Bonnie did not wish to pursue the matter, and they went on in silence for a while. They came to another spyhole, which looked on to a passage, and then they found themselves up against a blank wall. The secret corridor appeared to have come to a dead end.

Even Bonnie's heart sank, for the candles were perilously low, when they heard the clink of dishes, and a familiar voice, that of James, broke into song so close beside them that they might have been touching him.

"As I was a walking one morning for pleasure,
    I spied a young—"

"Knock on the wall!" Bonnie whispered to Sylvia, and both children began banging on the panel as hard as they could. The song broke off abruptly.

"James! James! It's us, in here behind the panel! Can you let us out?"

"Laws, miss, you gave me a fright," James's voice said. "I thought it was the hobgoblin for sure."

They heard him fumbling on the wall, and tapped again, to show him where they were. Suddenly there came a click, and bright cold light and icy air rushed into their hiding place.

"I always wondered why that great knob was there on the wall," James said. "Well, laws, miss! To think of your really finding the secret passage. That's champion, that is!"

They stepped out, and found themselves in the dairy, a brick-floored, slate-shelved room with several sinks, where some of the dishwashing was done. An outside door led from it to the stable yard, and they could see the whiteness of the new-fallen snow.

Since this entrance, too, appeared to have no means of opening it from the inside, James arranged to leave it open, artfully moving a tall cupboard so that it partly obscured the doorway, and hanging a quantity of horse blankets and other draperies to hide the remainder.

"Now at least no one need get shut up inside," said Bonnie. "The bother of it is that we can do nothing of the sort in the schoolroom. It would look too queer. The person in the passage will simply have to knock on the panel until somebody in the room lets them out."

"But supposing it was Miss Slighcarp in the room!"

"Goose! Of couse we should have to make sure before knocking that she was not in the room. I dare say there is a spyhole."

"Do you go back along the passage now and look," suggested Sylvia, "and I will return to the schoolroom by the back stairs and let you out."

This was agreed to, and Sylvia hastened away, glancing, as she passed the open door, at the stable clock to make sure that they would not be late for their meeting with Pattern. But it still lacked half an hour of five o'clock, the time appointed for the meeting.

Most unfortunately, as she neared the schoolroom door, she saw the gaunt, bony form of Miss Slighcarp approaching from the other direction, carrying in her arms a pile of linen. Sylvia was greatly alarmed when the governess swept before her into the schoolroom and deposited her burden on the table. What if Bonnie, not realizing that the governess was in the room, should have the imprudence to knock on the panel and ask to be let out of the secret passage?

"Now, miss," said Miss Slighcarp coldly—since the departure of her employers she had made no slightest pretense of being pleasant to either of the two children—"since I am at present too busy to occupy myself with teaching you, I have brought you a task so you shan't be idle. All these sheets and pillowcases require mending. To work at once, please!

If they are not finished by tomorrow you will come under my severe displeasure. Small stitches, mind."

"Yes, ma'am," said Sylvia, trembling, trying to keep her eyes from wandering toward the fireplace.

"I have a good mind to set that insolent child in the cupboard to this work too . . ." Miss Slighcarp muttered. She moved to the cupboard door, feeling in the reticule attached to the sash of her dress. Sylvia gasped with fright. "How very provoking! I gave the key to James." Sylvia let out a long, quivering breath of relief. "Miss Green!" the governess said, rapping on the door of the cupboard. "I trust you are repenting of your outrageous behavior?"

There was no reply from within the cupboard.

"Spirit not broken yet?" Miss Slighcarp moved away from the door. "Well, it will be bread-and-water for you until it is. On thinking the matter over, the light in that cupboard would not be sufficient to permit her to mend the linen."

This was no more than the truth, Sylvia reflected, for it must be pitch dark inside the cupboard.

Just as Miss Slighcarp was about to leave the schoolroom a loud, unmistakable rap sounded from inside the fireplace. Sylvia, pale with fright, sprang to the fender and began rattling the poker and tongs noisily, pretending to poke up the fire and put a few more pieces of coal on it. The governess paused suspiciously.

"What was that noise?"

"Noise, ma'am?" said Sylvia innocently.

"Something that sounded like a tap on the wall."

"It was this piece of coal, Miss Slighcarp, that fell into the grate." Sylvia spoke as loudly as she could, and rattled the fire irons more than ever. Miss Slighcarp seemed convinced, and left, after a sharp glance round to make sure that James had obeyed her command to pack up all the children's toys. Fortunately this had been done. The school-room and toyroom looked bleak and bare enough with all the gaily colored games and playthings removed, but Sylvia comforted herself by recollecting the hidden store up in the attic.

As soon as Miss Slighcarp was safely gone, Sylvia ran to the secret panel and with trembling hands pressed the carved deer's head, praying that she had remembered the correct prong on the antlers. To her unbounded relief the stone panel slid back as before, and Bonnie, black, dusty, laughing, and triumphant, fell out into her arms.

"Oh, is not this fun? Oh, what a narrow squeak! I had quite thought you were alone in the room, for neither of you had spoken for several moments before I tapped. Is it not provoking, there is no spyhole in this room? The first one looks out on the upstairs landing. But it is possible to hear voices from inside the passage, so long as somebody is speaking. What a mercy that you were so clever with the poker and tongs, Sylvia!"

Six

At five o'clock the two children stole cautiously to the little blue powder room, which, luckily, was in a remote wing of the great house, where Miss Slighcarp was not likely to make her way. Pattern was there already, and greeted them with tears and embraces.

"Oh, Miss Bonnie, Miss Sylvia, my dears! What's to become of us, that's what I should like to know, with that wicked woman in charge of the house?"

"*We* shall be all right," said Bonnie stoutly. "She can't do anything very dreadful to us, but oh, Pattern, what about *you?* She will have you sent to prison if she catches you here."

"She won't catch me," said Pattern confidently. "I crept in by the apple-room door when the other servants left, and I've fixed myself up in the little south attic on the fourth floor as snug as you please. My fine lady will never set foot up there, you may be certain. And I'll be able to creep down from there and help you with your dressing and put you to bed and look after your things, my poor lambs! Oh that I should live to see such a wicked day!"

"But Pattern, how will you live?" Bonnie was beginning, when James came quickly and quietly into the room.

"What a lark!" he said. "The old cat nearly caught me—met me in the long gallery—and asked what I was doing. I said, going to see all the windows were shut for the night, and she said, 'Yes, that's right, we want no thieving servants creeping back under cover of dark.' Thieving! I'd like to know what she thinks she is!"

The children told him Pattern's plan and he approved it heartily.

"For I don't trust Miss Slighcarp not to starve these young ones or do something underhand if we're not there to keep an eye on them," he said. "I'll look after their meals, Miss Pattern, if you see they're snug and mended and cared for. But, Miss Bonnie dear, you'd best write off to your papa's lawyer the very first thing, and tell him what's afoot here."

"But I don't know his address, James!"

"Eh, that's awkward," said James, scratching his head. "Who can you write to, then?"

"How about Aunt Jane?" Bonnie suggested to Sylvia. "She will surely know Mr. Gripe's address, for I have heard Papa say that Mr. Gripe is in charge of her money."

"Ye-es," said Sylvia doubtfully, "but Aunt Jane is so old, and so *very* frail, that I am afraid the news would be a dreadful, dreadful shock to her. It might make her ill, and then she is all on her own . . ."

"No, you are right," said Bonnie decisively. "It is not to be thought of. I know! We will write to Dr. Morne. He promised that he would come from time to time, in any case, so there would be nothing odd about asking him over. And very likely he will know Mr. Gripe's direction in London."

"Or perhaps he can get the magistrates to commit Miss Slighcarp to prison," said James. "That is a champion notion of yours, Miss Bonnie. Do you write the letter and I will ride over with it as soon as I get a chance."

"I will wait for a few days," suggested Bonnie, "just so

that Miss Slighcarp shan't be suspicious, and then will pretend to have the toothache."

A distant bell sounded, and James sprang up. "There! The old cat wants me for something and I must run. I'll be up to the schoolroom by and by with your suppers." And he hastened away.

Left with Pattern, the children told her how they had discovered the secret passage leading to the schoolroom, and she was delighted.

"I can come up that way to dress and undress you, and take your things away for washing," she said. "What a mercy of providence!"

"Only you must take care never to tap on the panel unless you are sure Miss Slighcarp is not in the room," Bonnie said chuckling.

"In any case, let us hope it need not be for long. Dr. Morne will soon settle her when you tell him what's going on here."

"Hark! There's the stable clock chiming the hour, Sylvia," said Bonnie. "I believe we should go back to the schoolroom so that presently James can come and let me out of the cupboard. It would be terrible if Miss Slighcarp were to accompany him and find me not there!"

During the next few weeks the children became half-accustomed to their strange new life. They hardly saw Miss Slighcarp and Mr. Grimshaw, who were too busy discovering what they could make away with from Sir Willoughby's property to have much time for the children. James and Pattern cared for them, bringing their meals and protecting them from contact with the other servants, who were a rough, untrustworthy lot. Several times the secret panel proved exceedingly useful when Miss Slighcarp approached the schoolroom on her daily visit of inspection, and Pattern, busy performing some service for the children, hastily darted through it.

There was little enough to do. They dared not be seen skating, and the snowy weather kept them near the house. But one day Prout, the undergroom, finding Bonnie crying for her pony in the empty stable, whispered to her that he had not sold the ponies, only taken them to one of the farms on the estate, and that when the weather was better they might go over there and have a ride. This news cheered Bonnie a good deal; to lose her pony, Feathers, and the new one that had been bought for Sylvia, on top of everything else, had been almost more than she could bear.

At last she decided that she could write to Dr. Morne without incurring suspicion. For a whole day she went about with her face tied up in a shawl, complaining that it ached, and that evening she crept up to the attic where her little desk was hidden and composed a note in her best handwriting, with advice from Sylvia.

Dear Doctor,

Will you please come to see us, as we don't think Papa would like the things that are happening here and we can't write to him for he is on board Ship. Miss Slycarp, our wicked Governess, has dismissed all the good old Servants and is making herself into a Tyrant. She wears Mamma's dresses and Mr. Grimshaw is in League with her and they drink champagne every Day.

Yours respectfully,
Bonnie Green and Sylvia Green

Alas! next morning when Bonnie gave James this carefully written note a dreadful thing happened. James had the note in his hand when he met Miss Slighcarp—who seemed to have the knack of appearing always just where she was not wanted—and her sharp eyes immediately fastened upon it.

"What is that, James?"

"Miss Bonnie has the toothache, ma'am. She wrote a note asking Dr. Morne if he would be so kind as to send her a poultice for it."

"I see. There is a heavy deed box in the library I want moved, James. Come and attend to it, please, before you deliver the note."

Unwillingly James followed.

"Put that note on the table," she said, giving Mr. Grimshaw, who was in the library, a significant look as she did so.

While James was struggling to put the heavy box exactly where Miss Slighcarp required it, under a confusing rain of contradictory instructions, Mr. Grimshaw quickly glanced at the direction on the note, and then, with his gift for imitating handwriting, copied the address on to a similar envelope with a blank sheet of paper inside. When James's back was turned for an instant he very adroitly exchanged one note for the other.

"There, then," said Miss Slighcarp. "Be off with you, sirrah, and don't loiter on the way or stop to drink porter in the doctor's kitchen."

The instant James was out of the room she opened the letter, and her brow darkened as she read it.

"This must be dealt with," she muttered. "I must dispose of these children without delay!" And she showed the letter to Mr. Grimshaw.

"Artful little minxes!" he exclaimed. "You are right! The children cannot be allowed to stay here."

"When can we move them? Tonight?"

He nodded.

James hurriedly saddled one of the carriage horses that

remained in the stable, armed himself with a pair of pistols in the saddle holsters and one stuck in his belt, and made off at a gallop for the residence of Dr. Morne, who lived some five miles beyond the park boundary.

Unfortunately when he reached his destination it was only to discover that the doctor had been called from home on an urgent case—a fire in the town of Blastburn in which several people had been injured—and was not expected home that evening. James dared not linger, though

he had been intending to reinforce Bonnie's note by himself telling the doctor how bad things were at the Chase. He could only deliver the letter and come away, leaving a message with the doctor's housekeeper imploring Dr. Morne to visit Miss Bonnie as soon as possible. Then he made his way homeward. A wolf pack picked up his trail and followed him, but his horse, its hoofs winged by fear, kept well ahead, and James discouraged the pursuit by sending a couple of balls into the midst of the wolves, who fell back and decided to look for easier prey.

The dull, dark afternoon passed slowly by. The children worked fitfully at their tasks of mending. Bonnie was no longer locked up, but Miss Slighcarp made it plain that she was still in disgrace, never speaking to her, and giving her cold and sinister looks.

The sound of a horse's hoofs had drawn both children to the window on one occasion, when Miss Slighcarp came suddenly into the room.

"Back to your work, young ladies," she said angrily. "Whom did you expect to see, pray?"

"I thought—that is, we did not expect—" Sylvia faltered. "It is James, returning from his errand."

"So!" Miss Slighcarp gave them again that strange glance, and then left them, after commenting unfavorably upon their needlework. She returned to the library, where she rang for James and gave him orders that utterly puzzled him.

"The carriage?" he muttered, scatching his head. "What can she want the carriage for, at *such* a time?"

Dusk, and then dark, came, and bedtime drew near. The children had long since abandoned their sewing and were sitting on the hearthrug, with arms entwined, in a somewhat sorrowful silence, gazing at the glowing coals which cast their dim illumination over the bare room.

"It is too late, I fear. Dr. Morne will never come today," Bonnie said sighing.

There was a gentle tap on the secret panel.

"Pattern! It is Pattern!" said Sylvia, jumping up, and she made haste to press the spring. Pattern came bustling out with a tray on which were two silver bowls of steaming bread-and-milk, besides little dishes of candied quince and plum.

"Here's your supper, my lambs! Now eat that while it's hot, and I'll be warming your beds and night things. Thank the good providence old Pattern's here to see you don't go to bed cold and starving."

When the last spoonful was eaten she hustled them into their warm blue flannel nightgowns, and saw them tucked up in bed. "There, my ducks! Sweet dreams guard your rest," she said, and gave each a good-night hug. At this moment they heard Miss Slighcarp's brisk heavy steps coming along the passage.

"Lawks-a-me!" gasped Pattern. She snatched up the tray and was through the secret door in a flash. Just as it clicked behind her Miss Slighcarp entered through the other door, carrying a lamp.

"In bed already?" she said. She sounded displeased. The children lay wondering what fault she could find with such praiseworthy punctuality.

"Well, you must just get up again!" she snapped, dumping the lamp on the dressing table. "Get up, dress yourselves, and pack a valise with a change of clothing. You are going on a journey."

A journey? The children stared at each other, aghast. They could not discuss the matter, however, as Miss Slighcarp remained in the room, sorting through their clothes and deciding what they were to take with them. Sylvia noticed that she put out only their oldest and plainest things. She herself was given none of the new clothes that Pattern had been making her, but only those made from Aunt Jane's white curtain.

"Wh-where are we going, Miss Slighcarp?" she presently ventured. Bonnie had such a behement dislike of the governess that she would never address Miss Slighcarp unless obliged to do so.

"To school."

"To school? But are you not then going to teach us, ma'am?"

"I have not the leisure," Miss Slighcarp said sharply. "The estate affairs are in such a sad tangle that it will take me all my time to straighten them. You are to go to the school of a friend of mine in Blastburn."

"But Mamma and Papa would never agree to such a thing!" Bonnie burst out indignantly.

"Whether they would or whether they would not is of no importance, young lady."

"Why do you say that?" asked Bonnie, filled with a nameless dread.

"Because I had a message this afternoon to say that the *Thessaly*, the ship on which your mamma and papa set sail, has been sunk off the coast of Spain. You are an orphan, Miss Green, like your cousin, and from now on it is I who have the sole say in your affairs. I am your guardian."

Bonnie gave one sharp cry—"Papa! Mamma!"—and then sank down, trembling, on the sofa, burying her face in her hands.

Miss Slighcarp looked at her with a strange sort of triumph, and then left the room, carrying the valise, and bidding them both be ready in five minutes.

As soon as she was gone, Bonnie sprang upright again. "It is not true! It can't be! She said it just to torment me!

But oh," she cried, "what if it is true, Sylvia? *Could* it be true?"

How could poor Sylvia tell? She tried to comfort Bonnie, tried to assure her that it must be lies, but all the time a dreadful doubt and fear lay in her own heart. If Bonnie's parents were no more, then their only protectors were gone. She thought with grief of cheerful, goodhearted Sir Willoughby and kind, gentle Lady Green. To whom, now, could they turn?

Before the five minutes were more than half gone Miss Slighcarp had come back to hasten them. With a vigilant eye she escorted them down the stairs and through a postern door to the stable yard, where the carriage was waiting, with the horses harnessed and steaming in the frosty night air.

Sleepy and shivering, they hardly had strength to protest when Mr. Grimshaw, who was there, hoisted each into the carriage, and then handed up Miss Slighcarp, who sat grimly between them.

"Well, a pleasant journey, ma'am," he cried gaily. "Mind the wolves don't get you, ha ha!"

"I'd like to see the wolf that would tackle me," snapped Miss Slighcarp, and then, to James on the box, "You may start, sirrah!" They rattled out of the yard and were soon crossing the dark and snowy expanses of the park.

They had gone about a mile when they spied the lights of another carriage coming toward them. It drew to a halt as it came abreast of them.

" 'Tis the doctor, ma'am," said James.

"Young ladies!" said Miss Slighcarp sharply. They caught sight of her face by the swaying carriage light; the look on it was so forbidding that it made them shiver. "One word from either of you, and you'll have me to reckon with! Remember that you are now going to a place where Miss

Green of Willoughby Chase is not of the slightest consequence. You can cry all day in a coal cellar and no one will take notice of you, if I choose that it shall be so. Hold your tongues, therefore! Not a sound from you while I speak to the doctor."

"Is that Miss Slighcarp?" the doctor called.

"Dr. Morne? What brings you out at this time of night?" She spoke with false cordiality.

"I received a strange message, ma'am—most strange, a blank sheet of paper, and an urgent summons to the Chase. Is everybody ill? Can nobody write?"

"Oh Doctor," she said, sweet as syrup, "I'm afraid it must be some prank of those dreadful children. They are *so* naughty and high spirited." (Here she gave both children a fierce pinch.) "There is nobody ill at the Chase, Doctor. I most *deeply* regret that you should have been called out for nothing. Let me give you ten guineas instead of your usual five."

There was a chink of coins as she leaned out of the dim coach and obscured the doctor's view of its interior.

He rumbled, dissatisfied. "Very odd, very. Can't say it's like Bonnie to do such a thing. Must be the other little minx. Don't care for being called out on false errands. However, very kind of you, ma'am. Say no more about it."

Still grumbling to himself, he turned his horses. Miss Slighcarp gave him a few minutes' start and then told James to make all possible speed toward Blastburn.

The rest of the journey passed in silence. Both children were utterly cast down at this failure of their plan, and Bonnie was almost numb with grief and despair over the news about her parents. Try as she would to control herself, tear after tear slipped from under her eyelids, and the utmost that she could achieve was that she wept in silence. She was too proud to let Miss Slighcarp guess her misery.

Sylvia guessed it, and longed to comfort her, but the bony bulk of the governess was between them.

Long before the end of the trip they were almost dead of cold, and their feet were like lumps of ice, for Miss Slighcarp had all the fur carriage rugs wrapped round herself, and the children had to make do without. They were too cold for sleep, and could almost have wished for an attack by wolves, but, save for an occasional distant howl, their passage was undisturbed. It seemed that Miss Slighcarp was right when she said that the wolves feared to attack her.

At last they drew near the great smoky lights and fearsome fiery glare of Blastburn, where the huge slag heaps stood outlined like black pyramids against the red sky.

They clattered through a black and cobbled town where the people seemed to work all night, for the streets were thronged, although it was so late, and presently drew up in a dark street on the farthest outskirts.

Miss Slighcarp alighted first, and Sylvia had just time to breathe hurriedly to James, as he lifted her down, "You'll tell Pattern where we are gone, James? She'll be so worried," and to receive his nod, before the governess pushed them along a narrow gravel path toward the front door of a high, dark house.

She rang a bell whose echoes they heard far within, harsh and jangling. Almost at once the door flew open.

Seven

The door was opened by a thin, dirty child in a brown pinafore with one white front pocket on which was stitched a large number six. Bonnie and Sylvia were not certain if the child was a boy or a girl until Miss Slighcarp said, "It's you, is it, Lucy? Where is Mrs. Brisket?"

"In here, please, miss," Lucy said with a frightened gasp, and opened a door on one side of the entrance hall. Miss Slighcarp swept through, turning her head to say to Bonnie and Sylvia, "Wait there. Don't speak or fidget." Then they heard her voice beyond the door:

"Gertrude. It is I. Our plans are going excellently." Somebody shut the door and they could hear nothing further. The little girl, Lucy, regarded the new arrivals for a moment, her finger in her mouth, before picking up a broom several inches taller than herself and beginning to sweep the floor.

"Are you a pupil here?" Bonnie asked her curiously.

The brown pinafore looked like some kind of uniform—but why was her hair cut so short, even shorter than a boy's? And why was she doing housework?

"Hush!" whispered Lucy. Her eyes flicked in terror toward the closed door. "She'll half kill me if she hears me speak!"

"Who?" breathed Bonnie.

"*Her.* Mrs. Brisket."

Bonnie looked as if she was on the point of asking more questions, but Sylvia hushed her, not wishing to get Lucy into trouble, and Lucy herself resolutely turned her back and went on with her work, stirring up a cloud of dust in the dim and stuffy hall.

Suddenly Sylvia had the feeling that they were being watched. She raised her eyes and saw someone standing by the banister rail at the top of the ill-lit stairs, staring down at them. Meeting Sylvia's eyes, this person slowly descended toward them.

She was a girl of about fifteen, tall and thin, with a pale, handsome, sharp-featured face. She walked with a slouch, and was very richly dressed in velvet, with a band of fur round her jacket and several bracelets. She carried a pair of silver skates.

She walked up to Bonnie and Sylvia, surveying them coolly and insolently. She made no remark or friendly gesture of greeting; merely looked them up and down, and then, with a sudden quick movement, tugged off Sylvia's white fur cap and tried it on herself. It was too small.

"Hm," she said coldly. "What a nuisance you're not bigger." She dropped the cap disdainfully on the floor. Sylvia's lips parted in indignation; even she, mild and good-tempered as she was, would have protested had she not noticed Lucy's face behind the girl's elbow, grimacing at her in an agony of alarm, evidently warning her not to object to this treatment.

Wordlessly, she picked up the beautiful white cap, its fur dusty from the heap of sweepings on to which it had fallen, and stood stroking it while the girl said carelessly to Lucy:

"Is my mother in there?"

"Yes, Miss Diana. Talking to Miss Slighcarp."

"Oh, *that* old harridan." She pushed open the door and they heard her say, "Ma, I'm going out. There's a fair, and all-night skating on the river. Give me five guineas." She reappeared in the doorway jingling coins in her hand, turned her head to say, "If either of the new girls is good at mending, make her sew up my satin petticoat. It's split." Then she pushed haughtily past them and went out, slamming the front door.

Miss Slighcarp summoned Bonnie and Sylvia to be inspected by their new instructress. As soon as they saw her they recognized the lady whom they had seen driving her carriage near the boundaries of Willoughby Chase. She was a tall, massive, smartly dressed woman, her big-knuckled hands loaded with rings flashing red and yellow, rubies and topazes. She glanced at the children irritably. Her eyes were yellow as the stones in her rings, yellow as the eyes of a tiger, and she looked as if she could be bad-tempered.

"These are the children, Gertrude," Miss Slighcarp said. "That one"—pointing to Sylvia—"is tractable enough, though lazy and whining and disposed to malinger. This one"—indicating Bonnie—"is thoroughly insolent and ungovernable, and will need constant checking and keeping down."

"I'm not!"

"She's not!" burst from Bonnie and Sylvia simultaneously, but Mrs. Brisket checked them with a glare from her yellow eyes.

"Speak before you're spoken to in this house, young ladies, and you'll get a touch of the strap and lose your supper. So let's have no more of it."

They were silent, but Bonnie's eyes flashed dangerously.

"Both, as you can see," continued Miss Slighcarp as if there had been no interruption, "have been grossly spoiled and overindulged."

"They'll soon have that nonsense knocked out of them here," said Mrs. Brisket.

Miss Slighcarp rose. "I am leaving them in good hands, Gertrude," she said. "I am very busy just at present, as you know, but when next we meet I hope *you* will be coming to visit *me*. You have helped me in the past, Gertrude, and soon I shall be in a position to help *you*."

She said this last very significantly. Bonnie's and Sylvia's eyes met. Was Miss Slighcarp intending to take complete possession of Willoughby Chase? Sylvia felt something like despair come over her, but Bonnie clenched her hands indomitably.

Mrs. Brisket ushered Miss Slighcarp out and saw her to the carriage. When it had gone, with a clattering of hoofs and a flashing of lamps, she returned to the children.

"We have no names here," she said sternly. "You," to Sylvia, "will be number ninety-eight, you number ninety-nine. Come, make haste, the others are in bed long ago except for the night workers."

She led them through the hall—where the little girl Lucy swept frenziedly as soon as Mrs. Brisket appeared, though it was plain she was dropping with sleepiness—and up flight after flight of steep, uncarpeted stairs. On the fourth floor she pushed Bonnie through a doorway, hissing, "The bed near the door," and raised the candle she carried long enough to show a large, bare room, crammed with small iron cots, on which children lay sleeping, sometimes two to a cot. One bed, by the door, was still vacant.

Sylvia had just time to whisper "Good night!" before she was hustled up to the floor above and thrust into a similar bedroom. She undressed in the pitch dark and fumbled her way into the bed, which was narrow, hard, and inadequately covered. "I'll never get to sleep," she thought, as she lay shivering miserably, trying to summon up courage to thrust her feet into the chilly depths of the bed. She could hear the mill hooters wail, and iron wheels clang on the cobbles; somewhere a church clock struck midnight. The whole of her short stay among the riches and splendors of Willoughby Chase seemed like a dream.

"Oh how I wish I was still with Aunt Jane," she thought unhappily. "But then I should not have met Bonnie, dear Bonnie!" She turned over, hugging the too-thin, too-narrow blanket round her. Suddenly a hand touched her cheek and a voice whispered, "Sylvia, is that you?"

"Bonnie!"

"I had to come and make sure you were all right."

Sylvia thought remorsefully how selfish she had been, lying and pitying herself while Bonnie had courageously dared the perils of the dark house to come and see her.

"Yes, I'm all right, quite all right!" she whispered. She reached out and hugged Bonnie. "Run back to bed quickly, someone may catch you!" She felt sure that in this place the punishment for getting out of bed would be dire.

"Just came to make sure," said Bonnie. "Don't worry, Sylvia, we'll keep each other company, it won't be too bad. And if we don't like it, well then we'll run away."

Though she said this so stoutly, her heart sank. Where could they run to, with Miss Slighcarp in occupation at Willoughby Chase?

"See you in the morning!"

"See you in the morning!"

With the memory of Bonnie's comforting presence, Sylvia at last found the courage to push her feet down to the cold bottom of the bed and go to sleep. But Bonnie lay awake for hour after hour, hearing the city clocks strike, and the wail of the factory hooters, and the rumble of wheels.

"What shall we do?" she thought again and again. "What shall we do?"

In the morning they discovered why the beds near the door were the last to be occupied. While the sky outside was still black as midnight and the frosty stars still shone, a tall girl thrust a great bell through the door and clanged it deafeningly up and down until every shivering inmate of the room had thrown back her covers, jumped to the floor, and begun dressing.

Dazed and startled, Sylvia nearly fell out of bed.

"Where do we wash?" she whispered to the girl by the next bed.

"Hush! You mustn't speak," the girl said, and pointed.

Sylvia saw a tin basin in one corner of the room, with a bucket beneath it. The biggest girl in the room broke the ice in the basin by giving it a sharp crack with her hairbrush, then they all washed in order of size. Sylvia was last. When it came to her turn there was no more than a trickle of dirty, icy water left in the basin. She could not bring herself to touch it. She was about to start plaiting her hair when the big girl who had washed first said:

"Wait, you! Julia, fetch the shears."

"Yes, Alice." The child who had told Sylvia not to talk ran from the room, and came back in a moment with an enormous pair of garden shears. Before Sylvia realized what was to happen, or had time to protest, Alice had seized hold of her pretty fair plaits and lopped them off, one after the other. Then she chopped the remainder of Sylvia's hair off as short as possible, leaving it in a ragged, uneven fringe round her head. There was no mirror in the room, so Sylvia could not see quite how bad it looked.

"What do you mean by cutting off my hair?" she gasped.

"Hush! It's the rule. Mrs. Brisket doesn't allow long hair. Now get into line."

The other crop-haired, overalled children were in line already. Alice pushed Sylvia into place at the back, took up her own position at the front, and led them downstairs. Sylvia caught a glimpse of Bonnie at the end of another line which joined theirs. Bonnie's hair, too, had been cut, and she, like Sylvia, had been given a brown overall to wear, with a number on the pocket. She looked almost unrecognizable, like a thin dark-haired boy. She gave Sylvia a wry grin.

The files had assembled round tables in a large, cold, stone-floored room. They stood waiting while three or four weary, grimy, exhausted-looking children, among whom was Lucy, brought round bowls which proved to contain thin, gray, steaming porridge. It was eaten without milk or sugar. After it they each had a small chunk of stale bread, with the merest scrape of dripping, and that was the end of breakfast.

At this moment Mrs. Brisket entered the room, and the whole school stood up. Mrs. Brisket said grace, and then looked sharply round.

"Where are the new girls?" she demanded. Bonnie and Sylvia were pushed forward from their places at different tables toward the rear of the room.

She scowled at them. "I am told that you left your beds and communicated last night. For that you will both miss your dinners."

Who could have heard them, Sylvia wondered. Then she caught sight of the big girl, Alice, who had cut off her hair. On Alice's rather lumpish, stupid face was a smug expression.

"Sylvia didn't do a thing! It was I who went to talk to her!" Bonnie exclaimed.

"Silence, miss! I will not have this insolence! You can miss your tea too. Perhaps that will teach you respect.

"Now, tasks. Number ninety-eight will work in the laundry. Eighteen, show her what to do. Ninety-nine, you will be in the kitchen, under cook. She will see that you don't give any trouble.

"There will be an inspection by the Education Officer this afternoon, so I want you all in the classroom at two o'clock sharp. Eighteen and ninety-eight, you must see that the night workers are waked in time."

She left the hall, and the children dispersed quickly and silently to their various tasks. Sylvia was led off by a thin, wiry, but quite friendly looking girl of fifteen or so, who whispered that her name was Emma.

"Don't we do any lessons?" murmured Sylvia.

"Hush! Wait till we're in the laundry, then we can talk."

The laundry was a large external room, stone-floored and bitterly cold, built out from the back of the house. It contained many large zinc washtubs, scrubbing boards, two huge iron wringers, and a great mound of coarse calico sheets and house linen waiting to be washed. Eight or nine other children came with them and set to work doggedly, sorting the linen and filling the tubs at an outside pump, the handle of which creaked so loudly that conversation could be pursued under cover of its noise.

"Don't, whatever you do, let *her* hear you talking," warned Emma. "We're only allowed to say necessary things to each other."

Her obviously referred to Mrs. Brisket.

Emma gave Sylvia a tub, a pile of sheets, and a bar of rough yellow soap.

"But do the parents allow their children to be made to work like this?" Sylvia asked in bewilderment.

"They are all orphans. This is a charity school, and Mrs. Brisket gets some money for running it. But as well she makes us do all the work, and take in outside work too. We do the washing for half Blastburn. Then when the

Education Officer comes round we go into the classrooms and pretend to be learning lessons."

"Do you like it here?" asked Sylvia, struggling to drag a bunch of heavy dripping cloth out of the cold water.

Emma glanced round cautiously, but no one else was very near, and the pump handle was going full blast. Leaning nearer she whispered:

"It's a horrible place! But don't let anyone hear you say so! The school is full of tale bearers. Everyone is always hungry—and Mrs. Brisket rewards anyone who carries her a tale against another person. She gives them a bit of cheese. She has a big laundry basket in her room full of bits of cheese, ready cut up."

So that was why Alice had reported on Bonnie's midnight visit. Sylvia herself, who was still just as hungry after breakfast as before it, felt her mouth watering at the thought of those bits of cheese.

When the sheets had been painfully scrubbed and rinsed three times by hands that were red and sore from the harsh soap and icy water, Emma showed Sylvia how to use the wringer.

"Never touch it with your hands. One girl lost her fingers in it. Now we always poke the sheets through with a stick."

She dumped the wrung-out sheets into a basket and carried them out to the yard behind the house, where there were long rows of henhouses and many washing lines. When the sheets were hung up, she and Sylvia returned to the central heap for a new lot.

The morning seemed endless. Sylvia was soon almost exhausted from the heavy work, and soaked through with icy water from the wringer, which sprayed anybody who was using it.

Presently the bell went for dinner. Sylvia had hoped that

as she and Bonnie were both to miss their meal, they might at least meet and talk somewhere. But she learned that people punished in this way were obliged to stand at the back of the dining room and watch everybody else eat. Mrs. Brisket sat at the head table eating grilled trout and plum pudding, and there was no chance to move a finger without being seen by her.

Bonnie looked tried and rebellious. She had a smear of coal dust on one cheek, a cut finger, and grease spots on her overall, but she grinned at Sylvia encouragingly. At the end of the meal she seized the moment when all the benches were noisily pushed back to whisper:

"It wasn't much of a meal to miss, anyway!"

Nor had it been. One thin slice of cold fat pork, a piece of beetroot, and a small withered apple.

After dinner Bonnie was summoned back to the scullery to help with the washing-up, while Sylvia and Emma went round with a bell to wake the night workers. Then Sylvia realized that, as the beds were insufficient for the number of children in the school, half of them slept by night and half by day. The night workers were always dropping with fatigue, as they were liable to be roused for duties in the daytime too, but just the same they were envied, as they performed their tasks without the fierce supervision of Mrs. Brisket.

It was a hard job to waken them. One by one they were clanged out of their slumbers and dragged from their beds. At two o'clock sharp the whole school, yawning and shivering, stood lined up in the heatless classrooms.

At half-past two Mrs. Brisket came round with the Inspector. The children were well trained. As the door opened into each classroom they burst out in chorus:

"A! B! C! D! E! F! G!" and so on, until the visitors had left.

In the next room it would be, "One! Two! Three! Four! Five!"

"Ah, I see they are getting on with their reading and arithmetic, ma'am," said Mr. Friendshipp, the Inspector, comfortably.

"Yes, Mr. Friendshipp. As you see."

"As I might have expected, in such a well-run establishment as yours, ma'am."

"And now, Mr. Friendshipp," said Mrs. Brisket, when they had passed through the last room, where Bonnie and Sylvia were standing, "come and have a small glass of port wine to keep out the chill."

After tea, which Bonnie missed, the children were set to mending. The meal had consisted of another small wedge of bread, dry this time, and a cup of water. Sylvia had contrived to save a half of her morsel of bread for Bonnie, and she pushed it into Bonnie's hand later, as they sat working in the biggest classroom, huddled together for warmth. This was the only time of day when they were allowed to talk to each other a little.

"The cook's a tartar!" whispered Bonnie. "If you say a word she hits you with the frying pan, or anything that's handy. And the kitchen is filthy—I'd sooner work in a pigsty. We can't stay here, Sylvia."

"No, we can't," breathed Sylvia in heartfelt agreement. "But how can we possibly get away? And where would we go?"

"I'll think of some plan," said Bonnie with invincible optimism. "And you think too, Sylvia. Think, for all you are worth."

Sylvia nodded. Then she whispered, "Hush, Diana Brisket's looking at us," and bent her head over the enormous rent in the satin petticoat which she was endeavoring to repair.

They had already learned that Diana Brisket was someone to dread. Her sharp eyes were everywhere, ready to catch the slightest fault, which she would then shrilly report to her mother, and her bony fingers were clever to prod or pinch or twist as she passed on stairs or landing. She was cordially hated by the whole school.

After they had sewed or mended for two hours they were put to sorting bristles for broom-making, while Mrs. Brisket read aloud a chapter of the Bible to them. Then there was supper—a choice of bluish skim milk or a cup of thin potato soup—and then they were sent to bed, most of them so bone-weary that in spite of hunger and the thin coverings they fell into bed and slept at once the dreamless sleep of exhaustion.

Eight

Bonnie did not last long in the kitchen. The second time that the cook hit her with the frying pan, Bonnie picked up a sauce boat full of rancid gravy and dashed it in the cook's face.

There was a fierce struggle, but the cook, one Mrs. Moleskin, a large, stout woman with a savage temper, at last thrust Bonnie into the broom cupboard and reported her to Mrs. Brisket.

Mrs. Moleskin was used to having a dozen terrified small slaves running hither and thither at her beck and call, and announced that she would not have Bonnie working under her. Accordingly, after a punishment which consisted of losing all her meals for two days, Bonnie was put on to doing the outside work, which was considered a terrible degradation.

In fact, she did not mind it half so much as being in the squalid kitchen. Outside work meant fetching in coal and kindling, lighting fires, sweeping the front and back steps, cleaning windows and doorknobs, digging the front garden, and looking after the poultry.

Bonnie, who was as strong as a pony, bore her two days' starvation with stoical fortitude. Twice Sylvia slipped her a piece of bread, but the second time she was caught by Alice, who snatched the bread and ate it herself, subsequently reporting the affair to Mrs. Brisket. Sylvia then had to forgo her own supper, and after that Bonnie would not let her sacrifice herself.

One dark, foggy afternoon when Bonnie, shivering in her thin overall, was sweeping snow off the front path, she suddenly heard a familiar whisper from the other side of the front railings.

"Miss Bonnie! Miss Bonnie!"

"Simon!" she cried out joyfully, almost dropping the broom in her surprise.

"Miss Bonnie, why ever are you doing work like that?"

"Hush!" breathed Bonnie, looking back at the house to make sure that Mrs. Brisket was not watching from one of the windows. "They've sent us to school here, Simon, but it's more like a prison. We can't stand it, we're going to run away."

"I should think so, too," said Simon with indignation. "Sweeping paths, indeed! And in that thin apron! It's downright wicked."

"But Simon, what are you doing in Blastburn?"

"Came in to sell my geese of course," he said winking cheerfully. "But to tell the truth, I was looking for you, Miss Bonnie. James and Pattern asked me to come. We was all uneasy about you and Miss Sylvia. What'll I tell them?"

At that moment a coal cart appeared and stopped outside the house. The coal man banged on the front door, shouting, "Coal up! Coal up! Coal up!"

Mrs. Brisket came out and ordered thirty sacks.

"Here, you," she said sharply to Bonnie. "Help the man carry them to the coal cellar. Who is that boy?"

She eyed Simon suspiciously.

"Geese for sale, geese for sale. Anybody want my fine fat geese?" he called, displaying the two geese he was carrying under his arms.

Mrs. Brisket's eyes lit up. She strode down the garden to the gate and prodded the two geese with a knowing finger.

"I'll give you five shillings each for them, boy."

"Ten!" said Simon.

"Ridiculous! Not a penny more than seven shillings!"

"Fifteen shillings the pair, ma'am—and it's a special price for you because I never can resist a handsome lady," said Simon impudently.

"Guttersnipe!" said Mrs. Brisket.

But she paid over the fifteen shillings and told Bonnie to put the two geese in the fowl run. In fact, the price was a ridiculously low one, as she well knew.

"I'll carry in your coal for a brown, ma'am," Simon suggested.

"Very well." She dug in her purse for another coin. "You can help the girl—the School Inspector is coming to dinner in half an hour, and I don't want children running to and fro and getting in the way when he arrives."

Simon picked up one of the sacks without more ado and humped it across the garden to the coal-cellar entrance, a flap door directly under Mrs. Brisket's drawing-room window. Mrs. Brisket unlocked the door and he tipped the coal down the chute and ran back for another load. By the time he returned Mrs. Brisket had gone indoors, leaving the key in the lock.

Simon glanced round to make sure that he was unobserved. The coal man, considering that his help was not necessary, had climbed back on to the seat of his cart and gone to sleep. Simon scooped a handful of snow aside and, pulling a knife out of his pocket, carved from the ground a hunk of yellow clay which he warmed and rubbed in his hands until it was soft. Taking the large key from the cellar lock, he pressed it vigorously into the clay, first on one side, then on the other, until he had two clear impressions of it. Then he put the key back in the lock, whipped off his muffler, damped it with snow, and wrapped it carefully round the lump of clay, which he placed under some bushes.

By the time Bonnie came running back from shutting up the geese, he was hard at work carrying his fifth sack of coal.

"Don't you try to carry one, Miss Bonnie!" he said with horror, as she went matter-of-factly to the cart. "They're far and away too heavy for you."

"I'll take them in the wheelbarrow," Bonnie said, and fetched it from the shed. "Mrs. Brisket would dock me of my supper if she looked out and saw that I was letting you do all the work."

"Does she do that?" Simon was horrified. "Does she starve you?"

"Not me," Bonnie said cheerfully. "I soon found out what to do. When she cuts one of my meals I make up on raw eggs. I didn't much like them at first, but when you're really hungry it's surprising what you enjoy."

"You mustn't stay here!" Simon exclaimed.

"Will you help us to run away, Simon?"

"That I will!"

"But, Simon, if we're to escape we shall need some clothes. That's what has been worrying me. She has taken our own things, and our purses with our money, so that we can't buy other things, and if we walked about in these overalls everyone would know that we were escaped from the orphan school."

"I'll bring you clothes," he promised.

"Boys' things would be best. I go to feed the hens every evening at six. You could meet me then, by the henhouses, as soon as you've got the clothes. If you went to Pattern, I'm sure she could give you something.

"The difficulty will be to get Sylvia out of the house, for she never has an excuse to come outside except in the morning when she's hanging up washing, and it would be too dangerous then."

"Wait till next week and I'll have a key made to get you out. Can you get into the coal cellar from inside?"

Bonnie nodded. "All too easily. She locks us into it as punishment quite often."

"Then I will give you a key to the outside door, and you will only have to contrive to be locked in."

Bonnie flung her arms round his neck. "Simon, you are wonderful! Now I must fly back or I shall be punished for loitering."

Simon watched until she had run indoors. Then he shied the last lump of coal to wake the driver of the cart from his beery slumbers, carefully took his piece of clay from its hiding place in the laurel bushes and, holding it as if it were the most precious gold, walked swiftly away to find the nearest locksmith.

Sylvia was obliged to miss her tea. She had been given a dress of Diana Brisket's to mend, and the task had taxed even her skillful needle, so disgracefully torn were its delicate flounces. Her head ached, and her cold fingers were less nimble than usual: consequently the dress was not finished when Diana wanted it. She flew into a passion, slapped Sylvia, and told her mother that number ninety-eight was lazy and refused to work. In consequence, Sylvia had to stand at the back of the dining room with the other wrongdoers at teatime, while Bonnie burned with sympathetic fury.

During sewing time after tea, Bonnie chose a moment when Mrs. Brisket was out of the room, crept round to Sylvia, and pressed something into her hand.

"Eat it, quick, before she comes back!"

Sylvia looked at what was in her hand and saw with amazement that it was a little cake, crisp and hot from the bakery.

"Where did you get it, Bonnie?"

"It must be from Simon! I found two of them in the nesting boxes when I went to collect the eggs. If I'd known that horrid wretch Diana would make you miss your tea, I'd have saved mine for you, too."

And she whispered to Sylvia the news of Simon's plan for them.

Sylvia was pale already, but she became paler still with excitement.

"Escape? Oh, Bonnie, how wonderful! Here, you finish this cake. I think I'm too excited to eat it." And she coughed.

"No, you must eat it, Sylvia. You had no tea."

"I can't, my throat is too sore. Where shall we go, Bonnie?"

"Well," Bonnie whispered, frowning, "we can't very well go back to Willoughby Chase, for they'd search for us there at once. And if James and Pattern tried to help us they'd get into trouble. What do you say to trying to get to London to see Aunt Jane?"

"Oh, Bonnie, *yes!* Dearest Aunt Jane, how I long to know if she is all right." Sylvia spoke with such enthusiasm that she coughed again. "But how shall we get there, Bonnie? It is such a long way, and we have no money for train tickets."

"I have thought of that. Very soon Simon will be driving his geese up to London for the Easter Fair at Smithfield Market. Easter falls at the end of April this year, and he will want at least two months to get there—"

"—And we could go with him!"

"Hush," whispered Bonnie, for at this moment the door opened and Mrs. Brisket re-entered the room.

She cast her usual suspicious glance round the assembled

113

children before beginning to read aloud from a volume of sermons, and they bent their heads and pretended to busy themselves over their work.

Every night that week, when Bonnie went to feed the hens and collect the eggs, her pleasantest task of the day, she felt a tremor of excitement. Would the key and clothes be there? But Tuesday, Wednesday, Thursday, and Friday evenings went by without her discovering anything unexpected in the henhouse.

On Saturday there was another inspection by the Education Officer, this time in the morning. He had really come to invite Mrs. Brisket to dine with him next day, but she always seized the opportunity of showing him how well-behaved and biddable her pupils were, and she had them all standing in rows for an hour before his arrival. The strain of this was too much for poor Sylvia. Drenched through every day with cold water in the icy, draughty laundry, she had taken a bad cold and was flushed, heavy-eyed, and feverish. Just as the Inspector entered the room where she stood, she fainted quietly away.

"That child, ma'am, is ill," said Mr. Friendshipp, pointing to her with his cane.

"Very likely it is all a pretense!" exclaimed Mrs. Brisket, looking at Sylvia with dislike. But on inspection it was plain that Sylvia's illness was genuine enough, and Mrs. Brisket angrily directed two of the big girls to put her to bed in a small room on the ground floor, where sick children were kept so that they should not give the infection to others. A basin of cold porridge was dumped in her room and, as she was much too ill to eat it, she would have fared badly had Bonnie not come to her aid.

Bonnie, discovering at dinnertime that Sylvia was missing, whispered to the friendly Emma to ask where she was.

"Ill, in the little locker room."

"Ill?" Bonnie turned pale. She had suspected for several days that Sylvia was ailing, though Sylvia always stoutly denied it.

If she was ill, how could they escape? On the other hand, if they did not escape, what would become of Sylvia? It was not impossible, Bonnie thought, that she might *die* of neglect and ill-attention in this horrible place.

With great daring Bonnie took a chance when Mrs. Brisket was inspecting the dormitories upstairs, and ran in to visit Sylvia, whom she found conscious, but dreadfully weak, flushed, and coughing. A cup of cold water stood by her bedside.

"Here!" whispered Bonnie, "here, Sylvia, swallow this down. It's not much, but at least it's nourishing and warm!" And she pulled from her pocket an egg, only five minutes laid, tossed the water from the cup out of the window, broke the egg into it, and beat it up with her finger.

"I'm sorry, Sylvia, that it's so disgusting, but it will do you good."

Sylvia gazed with horror at the nauseous mess, but Bonnie's bright, pleading eyes compelled her to swallow it, and it slipped more easily than she had expected down her sore throat. Then, hearing Mrs. Brisket descending the upper stairs, Bonnie covered Sylvia as warmly as she could, gave her a quick hug, and dashed silently away.

That evening, when Bonnie fed the hens and searched for eggs, she put her hand beneath one warm, protesting, feathery body and felt something hard and long among the eggs—a key! She pulled it out and found attached to it a label, which said, in Pattern's printed script:

"TOMORROW NIGHT AT TEN. LOOK UNDER THE STRAW BALES."

Bonnie ran to the bales of straw which were kept for the nesting boxes and found behind them two warm suits of clothes, a boy's, with breeches and waistcoat, and a girl's, with a thick woolen skirt and petticoat. Both were of coarse material such as tinker children wear, but well and stoutly made, and both had beautiful thick sheepskin jackets, lined with their own wool. In the pocket of each jacket was a golden guinea.

Bonnie guessed that the boy's was for her and the girl's for Sylvia.

"For Sylvia could never be got to look like a boy. Oh, how clever and good Simon is! He must have got Pattern to help him. But will Sylvia be able to travel? We *must* manage it somehow!"

She bit her lips with worry.

Snatching the opportunity while it was dark and there was nobody about, Bonnie carried the two bundles of clothes indoors and hid them in the coal cellar behind a large mound of coal while she was supposed to be filling Mrs. Brisket's evening coal scuttle and making up her fire.

During the evening she seized another chance to take a fresh egg to Sylvia and whisper the news to her. Poor Sylvia dutifully swallowed the egg and tried to be excited by the plan, but she felt so weak and ill that she was sure she would never manage the escape, though she dared not tell Bonnie this. Bonnie could see for herself, though, how frail Sylvia looked, and she became more worried than ever.

Sunday passed in the usual tasks.

Mrs. Brisket departed after ten to the party at Mr. Friendshipp's, leaving the school in charge of her daughter Diana, who, as her custom was, immediately began to bully and harry the children, making them fetch and carry for her, iron her clothes, curl her hair, and polish her shoes. Mrs. Brisket had forbidden her to leave the house, but she had no intention of staying in, and was proposing to visit a bazaar on the other side of the town, having calmly taken some money from her mother's purse.

"Here! You!" she called, seeing Bonnie hurrying past.

"Where are you going with that hangdog look? Come here!"

Bonnie came, as if unwillingly.

"What have you got in your pocket?"

Bonnie made no reply.

Diana thrust in her hand and let out a shriek of disgust.

She withdrew it and stared at her fingers, which were dripping with egg yolk.

"Thief! Miserable little thief! Stealing the eggs from my mother's henhouse!" She raised the dripping hand and slapped Bonnie's face with it.

Six months ago Bonnie would have slapped her back, and heartily, but she was learning patience and self-command. To be embroiled in a struggle with Diana was not part of her plan, though she longed to box the girl's ears.

"I was taking it to Sylvia," she said steadily. "Your mother is starving her to death. She has had nothing to eat all day but two raw onions."

"Is that any business of yours? Very well," said Diana, white with temper, "since you think you can look after Sylvia so well, you *shall* look after her. You can look after each other in the coal cellar. Alice, help me shut them in."

Alice, and a couple of the larger, worse-natured girls, willingly did so. Others remonstrated, as Bonnie was pushed, and Sylvia, still in her nightclothes, half-carried into the dark, dirty place.

"You shouldn't do it, Miss Diana. Sylvia's ill—it will make her worse," exclaimed Emma.

"Hold your tongue! Who asked *you* to interfere?" shouted Diana, and slapped her. The door was locked, and the key put in its accustomed place on Mrs. Brisket's parlor mantelpiece. Then, after making sure that everyone was in a properly cowed frame of mind, Diana wrapped herself in a velvet cloak and went out to the bazaar, locking the front door and taking the key with her.

Meanwhile Bonnie, in the coal cellar, was congratulating herself on the success of her idea as she swiftly helped to dress the trembling, shivering Sylvia in her new warm clothes.

"There, Sylvia! Now don't cry, there's a lamb, for I feel

sure Simon will have some good plan and will be able to take us to a place where you can be properly cared for. Don't cry!"

But Sylvia was too weak to hold back her tears. She sat obediently on a large lump of coal while Bonnie prepared to change her own clothes. But before she could do so there was a creaking of the lock and the door softly opened —not the door to the garden, but the one through which they had been thrust in. A head poked round it— Emma's.

"Bonnie! Sylvia! Are you all right? You can come out and get warm! Diana's out and Alice has gone to bed."

Bonnie felt the tears prick her eyes at this courageous kindness on the part of Emma. But how ill-timed it was! At any minute Simon might arrive, and she did not want anyone to know that he was helping with their escape.

She whispered to Sylvia, "Wait there, Sylvia, for two minutes, only two minutes, and then I'll be back," and ran swiftly to the cellar door.

Outside stood Emma and a large number of children, all deathly silent, in the passage that led from the kitchen. One of them pointed upward, meaning that they must make no sound for fear of Alice.

Bonnie was amazed and touched. She had had no idea how popular her bright face and friendly ways had made her with the other children, in the fairly short time she had been at Mrs. Brisket's.

Impulsively she hugged Emma.

"Emma, I won't forget this! If ever I get away from this hateful place" (and oh, I pray it will be tonight, she said to herself), "I'll send back somehow and get you out too. But Sylvia and I mustn't leave the cellar. If Mrs. Brisket or Diana came back you would get into dreadful trouble."

She looked at the children's anxious, eager faces and

wished that she could do something for them. Suddenly she had an idea. She ran to Mrs. Brisket's parlor and brought out the large hamper of cheese which the head-mistress kept for rewarding tale bearers.

"Here! Quick, girls! Eat this up!" She tossed out the chunks of cheese in double handfuls to the ravenous children.

"Cheese!"

"Oh, Bonnie!"

"Cheese!"

"Wonderful cheese!"

They had gobbled up most of the savory lumps before Emma suddenly exclaimed, "But what will Mrs. Brisket say?"

"I'll take care of that," said Bonnie grandly. She had been scribbling on a sheet of paper, "This is to pay for the cheese," and she now signed it with her name, fetched the guinea piece from her jacket pocket and put it with the paper on Mrs. Brisket's writing desk.

"There! She'll be angry, but she will see that I am the one to blame. Now, Emma, you must lock us up in the cellar again and put back the key. Yes!" as Emma protested, "I promise that will be best in the end," and she nodded vigorously to show that she meant it, and went back into the cellar.

With great reluctance Emma locked the door again. Instantly Bonnie flung off her brown overall and hustled on her boy's clothes, which felt very thick and strange, but comfortable.

"Oh, how funny I must look! I wish we could see ourselves. Here, Sylvia, I saved a piece of cheese for you. Try to eat it. It will give you some strength. We must take our aprons with us. It won't do to leave them behind, or they will guess that we have got other clothes and may be in disguise." She bundled them up and tucked them in her capacious pockets.

"Now for the key!"

Just for one awful moment it seemed as if the somewhat roughly made key would not open the outer door. However, wrapping a fold of her jacket over it and wrenching it with both hands, Bonnie got it round, and raised the flap. A gust of snowflakes blew into her face. "Good, it's snowing, so much the better. We shan't leave any footprints. Now, Sylvia, you had better have my coat as well as your own." She buttoned it on to her cousin, who was really too ill and weak to make any objection, and half-pulled, half-hoisted her up the slope down which the coal was poured. Then, swiftly, she relocked the door, put the key in her pocket, and urged Sylvia toward the gate with an arm round her shoulders.

"We can hide in a laurel bush," she whispered. "There's a thick one beside the front railings. Then if Mrs. Brisket or Diana should come back, they won't see us. I can hear the town clock striking ten—Simon should be here at any moment."

And indeed, as they reached the railings, they heard his voice whispering, "Miss Bonnie? Miss Sylvia? Is that you?"

"Yes, it's us!" Bonnie called back quietly, and ran to open the gate.

Nine

"Sylvia's ill!" Bonnie muttered to Simon as soon as they were outside the gate. "She can hardly walk! I think we shall have to carry her."

"No, she can go in the cart," Simon whispered back, and then Bonnie saw that he had with him a beautiful little cart, drawn by a donkey.

Her eyes lit up with delight. "Why, it's the very thing! Isn't it the one from Willoughby that we use for picnics—"

"Hush. Yes!" whispered Simon. "Let's get away quick, and then I'll explain."

Between them they lifted the trembling, shivering Sylvia into the cart. She gave a little protesting moan as she came into contact with something soft that seemed alive.

"What is it?" breathed Bonnie.

"The geese! They won't hurt her. There are quilts and mattresses underneath."

Swiftly and skillfully Simon disposed Sylvia in the cart, on a warm mattress, covered with several quilts. Thirty sleepy, grumbling geese were pushed unceremoniously to one side and then, when Sylvia was settled, allowed to perch all over and round her until only her face was showing.

"There! They'll keep her famously warm."

And in fact the warmth of the mattress and quilts and

the soft feathery bodies on top was such that in two minutes Sylvia was in a deep sleep, and never even felt the cart begin to move.

"Will you ride too, Miss Bonnie?"

"No, I'll walk at the head with you, Simon."

"Let's be off, then."

They hastened away. Simon had tied rags round the wheels and they went silently over the cobbled road. The only sound was the tippety-tap of the donkey's feet.

When they had turned several corners, and put several streets between them and Mrs. Brisket's school, both Simon and Bonnie breathed more freely.

"No one will remark us now," said Bonnie, as they passed into a wide, naphtha-lighted street in the middle of the town, where, although it was nearly midnight, trams still clanged up and down, and pit and factory workers trudged to and fro in their clogs.

"Certainly no one would take you for Miss Bonnie Green," said Simon, chuckling. "You make a proper boy in those things, haircut and all. Here, I brought these for you." He turned, sank an arm into the cart and rummaged among the geese, and brought out two sheep's-wool-lined caps, one of which he carefully placed over Sylvia's sleeping head. The other he gave to Bonnie, who gratefully pulled it on, for the snow was falling thick and fast.

"Miss Pattern made them for you; they weren't finished in time to leave with the other things."

"Pattern? Oh, did she make the clothes?"

"Yes, she did, when she heard I was going to help you, and James found the donkey and cart—Miss Slighcarp was going to have sold them, but James told her they belonged to parson and hid them away. I reckoned it would be just the thing for our journey. And Miss Pattern gave me a saucepan and a frypan and some cups and plates and a great pie—they're all in the back, under the seat. We'll have a bite to eat presently—I dare say you're famished, Miss Bonnie—but not till we're out of the town."

"Where is Pattern?" asked Bonnie.

"She's gone back to live with her mother at the lodge. She sent her dear love but didn't dare ask you to call in, for Miss Slighcarp passes there every day and there's only the one room, as you know. If there's a search for you they'd be bound to go there. It's best Pattern should not have seen you."

"And is James still at the house?"

"Yes. He gave me the guineas to put in your pockets out of his wages—and gracious knows they're little enough now."

"I've spent mine already, Simon," confessed Bonnie, and told what she had done.

Simon shook his head at her, but all he said was, " 'Twas like you, Miss Bonnie."

"Simon, it's ridiculous to go on calling me miss. Just call me plain Bonnie."

Simon grinned, but answered indirectly, "Have you got that coal-cellar key with you? Here's a good place to get rid of it."

They were crossing the bridge over the wide river, with its busy traffic of coal barges and wool wherries. When Bonnie produced the key and the two overalls, he made them into a bundle with a bit of string, weighted it with a cobble, and threw the whole thing into the river. Then they went on with light hearts.

The town presently gave way to country. Not much could be seen in the dark, but Bonnie caught dim glimpses of snow-covered slag heaps, with here and there a great pit wheel or chimney. Then they passed fields, enclosed in dry-stone walls. After a while they were climbing up a long, slow ascent, the beginning of the wolds.

"You'd best have a bit of a sleep now," Simon suggested to Bonnie after a couple of hours had passed. "We're safe away, and 'twill be morning by and by."

"What about the wolves, though?" Bonnie said. "Shan't we be in danger from them? I'd better help you keep a lookout. Have you brought a gun?"

"Ay, I've my bow, and James gave me your fowling piece. It's in the cart. But I doubt we'll not be troubled by wolves; it's turned March now, and with spring coming they'll be moving farther north. We're not likely to see any of them once we're over Great Whinside."

"What shall we do about Sylvia, Simon? She ought to stop somewhere till she's well enough for the journey."

"I've been thinking that, and I know the very place. We'll reach it about six in the morning. You get in the cart and have a nap now."

"All right, I will," said Bonnie, who was beginning to be very sleepy, "if you're sure the donkey can stand the load." She patted the donkey's nose.

"Caroline's pulled heavier loads than that."

So the cart was halted, and Bonnie, carefully, so as not to wake Sylvia, scrambled in and made a nest for herself among the feather quilts and the warm, drowsy geese. Soon she, too, was asleep.

When Bonnie woke she lay wondering for a moment where she was. There was no clanging bell, no complaining voices, and instead of shivering under her one thin blanket she was deliciously comfortable and warm.

A cool breeze blew over her face, the cart jolted, and then she remembered what had been happening and said softly, "Simon?"

His voice came from somewhere in front. "Yes?"

"Stop the cart a moment, I want to get out."

"Not worth it," he said. "We're nearly there."

Bonnie wriggled to a sitting position and looked about her. The sky was still mostly dark, but daylight was slowly growing in the east. Thin fronds of green and lemon-yellow were beginning to uncurl among masses of inky cloud. When Bonnie looked back she could see that they had come over a great ridge of hills, whose tops were still lost in the blackness of the sky to the north. Ahead of them was a little dale, and loops of the white road were visible leading down to it over rolling folds of moor. A tremendous hush lay over the whole countryside. Even the birds were not awake yet.

"That's where we'll have our breakfast." Simon pointed ahead. "That's Herondale. We're way off the main road now. No one's likely to come looking for us here."

He began to whistle a soft tune as he walked, and Bonnie, curling up even more snugly, watched in great contentment as the lemon-yellow sky changed to orange and then to red, and presently the sun burst up in a blaze of gold.

"Simon."

"What is it?"

"There's no snow here."

"Often it's like that," he said nodding. "We've left snow t'other side of Whinside. Down in Herondale it'll be warm."

Presently they came to the last steep descent into the valley, and Simon then allowed Bonnie to get out of the cart while he adjusted the drag on the wheels to stop it running downhill too fast. All this time Sylvia slept. She stirred a little as they reached the foot of the hill and walked through a fringe of rowan trees into a tiny village consisting of three or four cottages round a green, with a couple of outlying farms.

"We'll go to the forge," said Simon, and led the donkey across the green to a low building under a great walnut tree.

Bonnie fell back and walked beside the cart, smiling at Sylvia's puzzled, sleepy face. The geese were beginning to stir and stretch their long necks, and at first sight of them Sylvia looked slightly alarmed, but when she saw Bonnie she smiled too, and shut her eyes again.

"Smith's up," said Simon. A thread of smoke dribbled from the forge chimney, and they could see a red glow over the stable door in front, while the noise of bellows came in a regular wheezing roar.

Simon called over the forge door.

"Mr. Wilderness!"

The roaring stopped and there was a clink. Then a face appeared over the half door and the smith came out. He was an immensely tall man, wearing a blackened leather apron. Bonnie couldn't help smiling, he looked so like a large, gentle, white-haired lion, with a pair of dark eyes like those of a collie dog, half-hidden by the locks of white hair that fell over his forehead.

"Eh, it's you, Simon me boy? What road can I help you?"

"Caroline's loosed a shoe," said Simon, patting the donkey, "and as well as that we'd like your advice about the little lass here. She's not well."

"Childer come afore donkeys," Mr. Wilderness said. He moved over beside the cart and looked down at Sylvia's face among the geese. "Eh, a pretty little fair lass she be. What's amiss with her?"

"She's got a cough and a sore throat and a fever," explained Bonnie.

The smith gazed at Bonnie wide-eyed.

"And th'art another of em, bless me! Who'd ha' thought it? I took thee for a boy in that rig. Well, she's sleeping fair in a goose-feather bed, tha can't better that. Are they goose feathers?" he said to Simon.

"Stuffed the quilts and mattresses myself," said Simon nodding. "My own geese."

"Champion! Goose grease for chilblains, goose feathers for a chill. We'll leave her in the cart."

"Shouldn't she be put to bed?" Bonnie said doubtfully.

"Nay, where, lass? I've only the forge and the kitchen, where I sleep mysen. Nay, we'll put her, cart and all, in the shippen, she'll be gradely there."

He led them round the corner of the forge and showed them how to back the cart into a big barn with double doors on each side. When he opened these, sunlight poured into the place and revealed that it was half-full of hay, and lined along the walls with lambing pens made from hurdles. A tremendous baaing and bleating came from these and, walking along, Bonnie saw with delight that each pen contained a sheep and one, two, or three lambs.

"There's nought like lying wi' sheep two-three days for a

chesty cough," pronounced Mr. Wilderness. "The breath of sheep has a powerful virtue in it. That and a brew of my cherry-bark syrup with maybe a spoonful of honey in it, and a plateful or two of good porridge, will set her to rights better than the grandest doctor in the kingdom. Put her in the sun there, lad. When sun gets round we can open t'other doors and let him in that side. Now for a bite o' breakfast. I'm fair starved, and happen you'll be the same, if you've walked all the way fro' Blastburn."

"We've a pie and some victuals," Simon said.

"Nay, lad, save thy pie for later. Porridge is on the forge fire this minute, and what's better nor that?"

The geese had climbed and fluttered out of the cart, and were busy foraging in the hay. Bonnie, after making sure that Sylvia was well covered and had gone back to sleep, was glad to come into the smith's clean little kitchen, which opened off the smithy and was as warm as an oven. They sat down at a table covered with a checked red-and-white cloth.

Mr. Wilderness's porridge was very different from that served in Mrs. Brisket's school. It was eaten with brown sugar from a big blue bag, and with dollops of thick yellow cream provided by Mr. Wilderness's two red cows, who stood sociably outside the kitchen door while breakfast was going on, and licked the nose of Caroline the donkey.

After the porridge they had great slices of sizzling bacon and cups of scalding brown tea.

Then the smith prepared a draught of his cherry-bark medicine, syrupy golden stuff with a wonderful aromatic scent, and took it out to Sylvia, who was stirring drowsily. She swallowed it down, smiled a sleepy no-thank-you to an offer of porridge and cream, and closed her eyes again.

"Ay, sleep's the best cure of all," said Mr. Wilderness. "You look as if you could do wi' a bit too, my lass."

Bonnie did begin to feel that she could do nothing but yawn, and so Simon made her a nest in the hay and covered her with one of his goose-feather quilts. Here in the sun amid the comfortable creaking of the geese and the baaing chorus of the sheep she too fell into a long and dreamless sleep.

They stayed with Mr. Wilderness for three days, until he pronounced Sylvia better and fit to travel.

In the meantime Simon helped the smith by blowing the fire and carving wooden handles for the farm implements he made. Bonnie washed all his curtains, tablecloths, and sheets, and, aided by Simon, did a grand spring-cleaning of the cottage.

"Two months ago I shouldn't have known how to do this," she said cheerfully, beating mats on the village green. "Going to Mrs. Brisket's at least taught me housework and how to look after hens."

Mr. Wilderness was sorry to lose them when they went. "If tha'd ha' stayed another two-three weeks th' birds would ha' been nesting, and th' primroses all showing their little pink faces. Herondale's a gradely place i' springtime."

"*Pink* faces?" said Bonnie disbelievingly. "Don't you mean yellow?"

"Nay, they're pink round here, lass, and the geraniums is blue."

But even with this inducement they wanted to press on to London. They left with many farewells, promising that they would call in on the return journey, or come over as soon as they were safely back at Willoughby Chase.

The journey to London took them nearly two months. They had to go at goose pace, for in the daytime the geese flew out of the cart and wandered along as they chose, pecking any edible thing by the roadside, and, as Simon explained, "There's no sense in hurrying the geese or by the time we reach Smithfield they'll be thin and scrawny, and nobody will buy 'em."

"Anyway," said Bonnie, "supposing Mrs. Brisket and Miss Slighcarp have set people searching for us, the search will surely have died down by the end of two months."

So they made their leisurely way, picking flowers, of which they found more and more as spring advanced and they traveled farther south, watching birds, and stopping to bathe and splash in moorland brooks.

At night they usually camped near a farm, sleeping in or under the cart in their warm goose-feather quilts. If it rained, farmers offered them shelter in barn or haymow. Often a kindly farmer's wife invited them in for a plate of stew and sped them on their way with a baking of pasties and apple dumplings. In return, Sylvia did exquisite darning, Bonnie helped with housework, and Simon, who could turn his hand to anything, plowed, or milked, or sawed wood or mended broken tools.

Pattern had smuggled one or two books and Bonnie's paint box from the attic out to the cart with the food and clothes, and these were a great resource on rainy evenings in the hay. They read aloud to each other, and Simon, who had never bothered about reading before, learned how, and even pronounced it quite a handy accomplishment. He also took a keen pleasure in making use of Bonnie's box of colors, and sometimes could hardly be torn away from some view of a crag or waterfall that he was busy sketching. The girls would wander slowly on with Caroline, the cart, and the geese, until Simon, finished at last, caught them up at a run with the color box under his arm and the painting held out a arm's length to dry.

Sylvia and Bonnie thought his pictures very beautiful, but Simon was always dissatisfied with them, and would give them away to any passer-by who admired them. Several times people pressed money on him for them, and once, when they were stopping overnight in a little village named Beckside, the landlord of the inn, the Snake and Ladder, who had seen one of the sketches, asked if Simon would repaint his faded inn sign. So they spent a pleasant day at the village, feeding like gamecocks at the innkeeper's table on roast duck and apple cheesecake, while Simon painted a gorgeous green-and-gold serpent twined in the rungs of a pruning ladder.

"Should you like to be a painter, do you think, Simon?" Sylvia asked.

"I might," he confessed. "I'd never thought of such a trade before. Eh, though, but there's a lot to learn! And I doubt I'd never have the money for a teacher."

Bonnie opened her lips to speak, and then checked herself, sighing.

Late in April they came to the top of Hampstead Hill, among the gray old houses and the young green trees.

At the foot of the hill they could see the village of Chalk Farm, and, far away, the great city of London spread out, with its blue veil of smoke and its myriads of spires and chimneys. Sylvia felt a quickening of her heart to think she was so close to her dear Aunt Jane again. How pleased the old lady would be to see her beloved little niece!

They camped that night on Hampstead Heath near a tribe of gypsies—and indeed they looked like gypsies themselves. Bonnie and Simon were as brown as berries and their black locks were decidedly in want of cutting, while even Sylvia would hardly have been recognized for the thin, pale, fair child who had set out to Willoughby Chase so many months ago. Her cheeks were pink, and her hair, though not its original length yet, was thick and shining and reached to her shoulders.

They found an obliging dairyman in Hampstead Village

who was willing to keep Caroline and the cart for them in his stable, and next day they drove the geese down into London.

"You girls had best not come to Smithfield Market," said Simon. "It's a rough, wild place, not fit for little maids."

"I've been thinking," suggested Bonnie, "how would it be if we tried to find Mr. Gripe's office while you are at the Market? Sylvia, can you tell us where lawyers' offices in London are usually to be found?"

Sylvia said she thought they were in the region of Chancery Lane. Having inquired the way of a constable, therefore, the girls accompanied Simon as far as Lincoln's Inn Fields, and there he left them with Goosey and Gandey, the two parent geese, who were never sold, while he went on to dispose of the rest of the flock.

Bonnie and Sylvia wandered along outside the houses that surrounded the Fields and saw on brass door plates the names of many attorneys, barristers, and Commissioners for Oaths, but nowhere that of Mr. Gripe.

At about midday when, tired, they were lying sunning themselves on the grass, and eating sliced beef and lemon tarts procured at a nearby cookshop, Bonnie suddenly exclaimed:

"Look, Sylvia, look! Isn't that Mr. Grimshaw?"

A portly, middle-aged man was walking across the grass toward a nearby archway. Sylvia scrutinized him closely and whispered:

"Yes! I am almost sure it is he! If he would but turn his head this way!"

"We must follow him and find out," Bonnie said decisively. "If he, too, is in London we shall have to be on our guard."

The two children got up and, calling their geese, walked fast, but not so as to attract his attention, after the gentleman in question. He passed through the archway, descended some steps, and turned into a small street, where he stopped outside one of the houses.

"Perhaps it is his residence," whispered Sylvia.

They approached slowly. Unfortunately a large black cat was seated on the pavement, and if there was one animal that Goosey abominated, it was a cat. He sat up a vociferous honking and cackling, and the gentleman, in the act of ringing the doorbell, turned his head and looked at the two girls. His eyes passed over Bonnie, but he stared very sharply at Sylvia for an instant—then the door opened and he was admitted.

"Oh mercy!" exclaimed Sylvia, "do you think he recognized me? For it was *undoubtedly* Mr. Grimshaw! I could not have sat so long opposite him in the train and been mistaken."

"I am not certain if he knew you," said Bonnie uneasily. "It is possible. You are not so sunburned as Simon or I. We had better not remain in this vicinity."

They were turning to go when Bonnie's quick eyes caught sight of the brass plate by the door that Mr. Grimshaw had entered.

"Look Sylvia! Abednego Gripe, Attorney. Father's man of business! Is not that a lucky chance!"

"Is it so lucky?" said Sylvia doubtfully, as they retraced their steps along the street. "I do not like the fact that Mr. Grimshaw has gone to see him. Why can he have done so, do you suppose?"

"No, you are right," Bonnie answered thoughtfully. "It is very queer. At all events, we must not go to see Mr. Gripe while Mr. Grimshaw is there. We had best wait until we have seen Aunt Jane and asked her advice."

They remounted the steps and saw Simon crossing Lincoln's Inn Fields. He waved to them triumphantly.

"Twenty-two pounds, girls! They fetched fourteen and eightpence each!" he called as soon as he came within earshot. "We are rich!"

"Heavens, what a lot of money!" breathed Sylvia.

"Let us be off to Aunt Jane at once," said Bonnie.

"Shall you want me to come?" asked Simon diffidently.

"Gracious, yes! Why ever not?"

"I'm only poor and rough—"

"Oh, what nonsense," said Bonnie, seizing his hand. "You can't come all this way with us and then desert us now, just when things might turn out better! Sylvia, tell us how to get from here to Park Lane."

They finished their four-hundred-mile journey riding on the open upper deck of one of the new horse-drawn omnibuses, geese and all, though Sylvia did rather shudder to think what Aunt Jane would say to this, should she chance to be looking out of her window when they arrived. Aunt Jane had many times told Sylvia that *no* lady *ever* rode in an omnibus, and more particularly not on the upstairs deck.

"I feel half-afraid," confessed Sylvia, laughing, looking up at the familiar tall house with its Grecian columns on either side of the door and white window boxes filled with lobelia. "Look, Bonnie, that is our window—the attic one, right up in the roof."

"The window-box flowers are withered," commented Simon.

"So they are. That is not like Aunt Jane," said Sylvia, puzzled. "She usually waters them so carefully."

The main door to the house stood open, and they went in silence up the stairs—up, up again, and still up. As they passed a door on the fourth-floor landing, it flew open and a young man's head popped out exclaiming, "Is that the grocer? Have you brought my pies and turpentine? Oh—" in disappointment, as he saw Simon and Bonnie and the geese.

Sylvia had impatiently gone on ahead. The young man eyed them in surprise a moment, then shut his door again.

They caught up with Sylvia on the top landing. She was already tapping at Aunt Jane's attic door.

"It is strange! She does not answer!"

"Perhaps she's out shopping?" suggested Simon.

"But she always takes tea at this time of day." (It was five o'clock.)

"She could not have moved away?" Bonnie said with a sinking heart.

"No," exclaimed Sylvia in relief, "here is the spare door key that she always keeps under the oilcloth in case by some mischance she should lose her other one. She must be out, after all. We will go in and surprise her on her return."

She opened the door with the key, and, cautioning them by laying her finger on her lips, tiptoed in. Bonnie and Simon rather shyly followed and stood hesitating in the tiny hallway, while Sylvia went on into the one room which served Aunt Jane for kitchen, parlor, and bedroom.

Suddenly they heard Sylvia give a faint cry, and she came back to them, white and frightened.

"What is it, Sylvia?" said Bonnie anxiously.

"It is Aunt Jane! Oh, I think she must be dreadfully ill, or in a faint—she is there, and so thin and pale and hardly breathing! Come, come quickly!"

They hastened after her, Simon pausing but a moment to shut the geese out on the landing. They saw the poor old lady stretched on her bed under the jet-trimmed mantle. Her eyes were closed, and her breathing was rapid and shallow. "Aunt Jane?" whispered Sylvia. "It is I, Sylvia!" There was no reply.

Ten

All three children retreated on to the landing once more. It seemed dreadful to stay in the little close room and talk about Aunt Jane with her quite unconscious of their presence. Sylvia noticed that the window was shut, the dishes unwashed. A thick layer of dust covered everything.

"What do you think is the matter with her?" Sylvia said, her voice quavering.

"I don't know," said Bonnie decidedly, "but whatever it is, we must get a doctor to her at once."

"Yes, Bonnie, how sensible of you! But where shall we find one?"

"Has Aunt Jane no regular doctor?"

"She always said she could not afford one," said Sylvia, dissolving into tears. "She always said all her ailments could be cured by P-Parkinson's Penny Pink Pills."

"Now come, Sylvia, don't get into those crying ways again," Bonnie began, sounding cross because she was so worried, when Simon interposed:

"I think I saw a doctor's plate on the floor below. Wait a moment and I'll go down and make certain."

He pushed past the geese, who were roosting on the stairs, and ran down to the landing below. Sure enough, by the door out of which the head had popped was a notice: GABRIEL FIELD—physician and chirurgeon.

Simon knocked. A voice shouted, "Come in, it's not locked," and so he pushed open the door and looked into a room which was in a considerable degree of confusion. Several shelves along the walls bore a clutter of bottles, phials, and surgical implements; a large table was covered with brushes, jars, and tubes of paint, while the floor was almost equally littered with stacks of canvases and piles of medical books.

The young man who had looked out before stood with a paint brush in his hand, considering a half-finished painting on a large easel.

"Oh, it's you again, is it?" he said, seeing Simon's perplexed face round the door. "What d'you want?"

Simon found something reassuring in his rather brusque manner.

"Please, are you Dr. Field, sir?"

"Yes, I am."

"The old lady upstairs is very ill. Could you come and look at her?"

"Certainly. Just a moment while I wash my hands."

While Dr. Field was washing, and fetching a black bag of medicines from his bedroom, Simon stared at the picture on the easel.

"Like it?" said the doctor, coming back.

"Yes," said Simon. "I do, very much. But I'm not sure about this bottom right-hand corner. It seems a bit too dark."

The doctor gave him a surprised look before waving him out of the door and hurrying upstairs. He brushed past the two girls and the geese without comment, and made his way in to Aunt Jane's bedside. "One of you two girls come and help me," he said, so Sylvia went, while the other two remained on the landing in a silence of anxiety and suspense.

They had to wait some time, while Dr. Field made a thorough examination of Aunt Jane. Then he and Sylvia came out on to the landing again.

"She's your aunt, is she?" he said sharply. "Well, you've been neglecting her. She's suffering from malnutrition." As none of them appeared to understand this word he added impatiently, "Undernourishment. She's been starving herself."

Sylvia began to cry quietly.

"Oh, poor, *poor* Aunt Jane! I should never half left her."

"I'm to blame, too," said the doctor angrily. "I saw her coming upstairs, a couple of weeks ago, with her shopping —one egg and an apple. I should have guessed."

"What does she need, sir?" said Simon quietly. "I'll go out and get it."

"Firstly, champagne. She's too weak to take anything else at the moment. You needn't bother about that, I've a bottle in my room. Then beef tea, eggs, milk, butter, honey."

"We'll go and get them," said Bonnie. "Come on, Simon. I saw a basket in Aunt Jane's parlor. Sylvia, you stay with the doctor and see to the champagne. Can you direct us to the nearest market, sir? We have only just come to London and don't know our way about."

Dr. Field told them how to find the nearest market, and they ran off with their basket, while Sylvia helped administer a few teaspoonfuls of champagne to Aunt Jane, tipping it between her motionless lips.

"You're the old lady's niece, are you?" the doctor said. "I've only been in this house a month. I thought she had no kin at all. It's high time she was properly looked after."

Sylvia considered the doctor. He had a kind, sensible face, and she was inclined to confide the whole story to him and ask his advice, but thought she had better wait till the others returned.

Simon and Bonnie soon came back. They were loaded, for, as well as the food, Simon was carrying a small sack of coal, and Bonnie had a blanket and a fleecy shawl.

While they were out they had had a short, brisk argument.

"Simon, this is your money we're spending—your year's money. We shouldn't be doing it."

"Oh, fiddlesticks!" he said uncomfortably. "Anybody would do all they could to help that poor old lady."

"Well, I shall pay you back as soon as I possibly can, Simon, if I ever get my own home and money back, but otherwise you do understand you'll have to wait till I can earn some money, and gracious knows how many months that will be!"

"Oh, get along with you, girl, you're wasting time," said Simon good-naturedly.

Dr. Field suggested that they should do their cooking downstairs in his room in order not to disturb the invalid, so Bonnie, first borrowing Aunt Jane's cookery book, set about scraping some beef and putting it to simmer with carrots and a teaspoonful of brandy. Simon lit a fire in Aunt Jane's room, and Sylvia tiptoed about cleaning the place and setting it to rights. Every now and then Dr. Field came and administered another teaspoonful of champagne, and presently he reported with satisfaction an improvement in the patient's breathing and a tinge of color in her cheeks.

"Your cousin's cooked you a meal," he said to Sylvia and Simon after a while. "Better come down and eat it in my room."

They realized they had not eaten all day, and were glad to come down. Bonnie had cooked a great panful of bacon and eggs, which she cordially invited the doctor to share.

"Are you all cousins?" said he, when they were eating, among the paints and bottles of medicine.

"Oh no. Sylvia and I are, but Simon's no relation."

"Where are all your parents?"

They looked at each other, and, without the need for discussion, decided that they could trust the doctor. Bonnie told him the whole story, ending with the sight of Mr. Grimshaw at the lawyer's office that morning. "And oh, sir," she ended, with tears in her eyes, "can you tell me if the ship my parents sailed in truly sank? *Truly?*"

"What was its name?"

"The *Thessaly*."

"Yes, my poor child," he said sadly. "I wish I could tell you otherwise, but I read the report in *The Times* myself. It was said that the captain should never have set sail, knowing the dangerous state of the ship's hull. It was said that someone must have paid him handsomely to do so, and it was rumored that he himself had escaped in a small boat, some hours before the wreck."

Bonnie could not speak for a moment. She turned away to the window and bit her lip.

Dr. Field went on hastily to break the unhappy silence:

"The whole business sounds to me like a plot, hatched up beforehand between this Miss Slighcarp of yours, who's evidently a thorough wrong 'un, and her precious friends Grimshaw and Mrs. Brisket. Whether Gripe the lawyer has a hand in it too we can't be sure, but I've a friend who's a lawyer, and as soon as old Miss Green's fit to be left I'll go and see him, and ask him what he knows about Gripe."

"Oh, *could* you, sir? Thank you indeed."

Their faces of gratitude evidently touched his heart, for he said gruffly, "A couple of you can bed down here if you like. I've plenty of cushions. Just shift some of those books and pictures and the skeleton off the sofa." (Sylvia gave a faint scream. She had not noticed the skeleton before.) "One of you should sleep upstairs with the old lady. And you'd

142

better all get yourselves a wash and brush-up. You look as if you can do with it."

The beef tea was ready now, and Sylvia, with the doctor's help, fed some of it to Aunt Jane through a straw. She opened her eyes once or twice, but seemed hardly conscious of her surroundings yet.

With the aid of a couple of the doctor's blankets Sylvia made herself up a couch for the night by the side of Aunt Jane's bed. They were all tired, and went to sleep as soon as they lay down.

In the middle of the night Sylvia awoke. She had left a night light burning, and by its faint glimmer she saw that Aunt Jane had raised herself on her pillows and was looking wonderingly about her.

"Mind, Auntie," said Sylvia, springing up. "You'll uncover yourself!"

Carefully she arranged the woolly shawl round her aunt's shoulders again.

"It *is* Sylvia! But no," said Aunt Jane mournfully. "I have so often dreamed that she came back. This must be just another dream."

"No it isn't!" said Sylvia, forgetting to be careful in her joy and giving her aunt an impetuous hug, "it really is me, come back to look after you. And I've brought Bonnie too."

"Sylvia, my precious child," Aunt Jane murmured, and two tears slipped down her cheeks.

"Now, Aunt dear, you *mustn't!* You must get strong quickly. Please try to sip some of this," said Sylvia, who had been hastily heating up the beef tea over the night light.

Aunt Jane sipped it, and soon, for she was still very weak, she slipped off to sleep, holding Sylvia's hand. Sylvia, too, began to doze, leaning against her aunt's bed, half-wake and half-dreaming.

She dreamed that she was on top of a mountain, the black

ridge that they had crossed before they reached Herondale. She saw Miss Slighcarp coming up from Blastburn at the head of a pack of wolves. Sylvia was dumb with fright. She was unable to move. Nearer and nearer Miss Slighcarp came, tramp, tramp, tramp . . .

Suddenly Sylvia was awake. And listening. And there *were* footsteps coming up the stairs.

She lay palpitating, with her heart hot against her ribs. Who could it be? The night was still black dark. No light showed under the door. If it was the doctor, surely he would be carrying a light? The steps were very slow, very cautious, as if whoever it was wanted to make as little sound as possible. Sylvia knew that she must move—she *must*—

A frantic cackling, hissing, and honking broke out on the stairs. There was a yell, a thud, more cackling, pandemonium!

"What is it?" said Aunt Jane drowsily.

"Oh, what can it be?" cried Sylvia, pale with terror. But the noise had shaken her out of her paralysis, and she seized a candle, lit it at the night light, and ran to the door.

The scene that met her eyes when she held the door open was a strange one. At the top of the stairs were two indignant geese, still hissing and arching their necks for battle. Prone on the stairs, head down, and cursing volubly, was Mr. Grimshaw. Simon held one of his arms and Bonnie the other.

Dr. Field, in a dressing gown, looking sleepy and considerably annoyed, was emerging from his front door holding a piece of rope, with which he proceeded to tie Mr. Grimshaw's hands and ankles.

"Breaking into people's houses at three in the morning," he muttered. "That's really a bit high! It's bad enough having children and geese camped all over the place."

"It was lucky the geese sounded the alarm," said Bonnie, pale, but clutching Mr. Grimshaw gamely.

"True," Dr. Field agreed. "Now, lock him in the broom closet. Good. I'll just run down and bolt the outside door, then perhaps we can have a bit more sleep. We'll get to the bottom of all this in the morning."

Yawning, they all went back to bed, but Sylvia declared she was too scared to sleep without Bonnie, and so they brought up more of the doctor's cushions and made a double pallet beside Aunt Jane's bed.

Eleven

Dr. Field's face at breakfast next morning was grim, and the children were all rather silent. The unseen presence of Mr. Grimshaw in the broom cupboard put a damper on their spirits.

"What do you suppose he was trying to *do?*" whispered Bonnie.

"Oh, very likely just see if you were there," said Dr. Field doubtfully. "Or try to frighten the old lady into handing you over if you should turn up later. At all events, you and the geese between you put an effective stop to him. I shall take him straight to Bow Street after breakfast and put him in charge of the constables."

Luckily Aunt Jane was a great deal better this morning. After the doctor had inspected her, he pronounced that she might be given a little warm gruel and some tea and dry toast, which Bonnie and Sylvia prepared. Aunt Jane greeted Bonnie kindly and declared that she would never have recognized her—which was very probable, as the last time she had seen Bonnie had been at her christening. Then Sylvia announced that she would remain with the old lady while the rest of the party went off with the prisoner; the very sight of Mr. Grimshaw, she said, made her feel sick with fright. Dr. Field considered this to be a sensible plan, and he told Simon to go out and whistle for a hackney cab.

Mr. Grimshaw was released from his closet, but his bonds were not untied. He was sulky, threatening, and lachrymose by turns; in the same breath he begged for mercy and then swore he would get even with them.

"That's enough, my man. You can spare your breath," said Dr. Field, and showed him a blunderbuss, ready primed, which he had taken of out of his desk drawer. At sight of this weapon Mr. Grimshaw relapsed into a cowed silence.

"Shall I get my fowling piece?" exclaimed Bonnie, and then remembered that it was with the cart in Hampstead.

Dr. Field looked slightly startled but said he thought one weapon should be sufficient to keep the scoundrel in order.

At this moment Simon came back to report that a cab was waiting below, and after a solicitous farewell to Aunt Jane and Sylvia, bidding the latter keep the door locked and admit nobody, they took their departure.

At Bow Street they waited only a very few minutes while the doctor haled his prisoner into the Constabulary Office; he soon reappeared, accompanied by a couple of burly, sharp-looking individuals who marched Grimshaw between them, and they all piled into the cab again.

"Where is he to be taken now?" said Bonnie.

"We shall go to Mr. Gripe's office for some explanation of Grimshaw's behavior," Dr. Field told her. "He has said that he worked for Mr. Gripe."

They were soon back in the region of Lincoln's Inn Fields, and drove up to the house that Bonnie and Sylvia had seen the day before. A scared-looking clerk, hardly more than a boy, admitted them into a waiting room, and next moment a thin, agitated, gray-haired man hurried into the room, exclaiming, "What can I do for you gentlemen? I am Abednego Gripe."

He appeared excessively surprised to see the children and

the manacled Mr. Grimshaw. Bonnie soon decided that he could not have hatched a dark plot to obtain possession of Willoughby Chase—he looked too kind and harmless.

One of the Bow Street officers spoke up.

"I am Sam Cardigan, sir, an officer of the constabulary. Here is my card. Can you identify this person here?" indicating Mr. Grimshaw.

"Why yes," said Mr. Gripe, looking at Mr. Grimshaw with distaste. "His name is Grimshaw. He was a clerk in my office until he was dismissed for forgery."

"Aha!" said the other Bow Street officer, whose name was Spock.

"Have you ever seen him since you dismissed him?" said Dr. Field.

"No indeed. He would have a very cold reception in this office."

"And yet he was seen entering here yesterday," snapped Cardigan.

Mr. Gripe seemed surprised. "Not to my knowledge."

Cardigan looked thunderously disbelieving and was about to burst out with his suspicions of Mr. Gripe, when the little clerk who had let the party in, and who had been standing in the doorway with eyes like saucers, piped up:

"Please, sir, I saw him."

Mr. Grimshaw darted a furious look at this speaker.

"Who are you?" said Cardigan.

"Please sir, Marmot, a clerk. Yesterday while Mr. Gripe was out having dinner, th-that gentleman as is tied up there came and asked me to give him the address of Miss Jane Green, sister to Sir Willoughby."

"And you gave it him?"

"Yes, sir. He said he wished to take her some dividends."

"Dividends, indeed!" growled Dr. Field. "Wanted to murder her more probably."

"Certainly not," said Grimshaw, pale with fright. "I merely wished to ascertain from her if these children, who are the runaway wards of a friend of mine, had taken shelter with her."

"At three o'clock in the morning? A fine story! More likely you wanted to terrify her into signing some document giving you power over the children. And what about this Letitia Slighcarp?" continued Dr. Field, glaring at the lawyer. "Were you responsible for sending that female fiend to feather her nest at Willoughby Chase?"

Mr. Gripe looked very much alarmed. "She is a distant relation of Sir Willoughby. She came with the highest references," he began. "From the Duchess of Kensington. I have them still." He pulled out a drawer in a cabinet and produced a paper. Cardigan scanned it.

"A patent forgery," he said at once. "I have seen the Duchess's signature on many documents and it is utterly unlike this."

"Then I have been duped!" cried Mr. Gripe, growing paler still. "But what can have been the object of this deceit?"

"Why," said Bonnie indignantly, "Miss Slighcarp has taken our whole house for her own, dismissed all the servants, sent me and my cousin to live in a school that is no better than a workhouse or prison, and treated us with miserable cruelty! And I believe, too, she and Mr. Grimshaw had some hand in seeing that Papa and Mamma set sail on a ship that was known to be likely to sink!"

"This is a bad business, a very bad business," said Mr. Gripe.

"No, no!" cried Mr. Grimshaw, now nearly dead of terror. "We were not responsible for that! The ship was sunk by an unscrupulous owner to obtain the insurance. It was when I learned—through a friend who was a shipping clerk

—that they were to sail on the *Thessaly*, that the plan took shape. I had seen Sir Willoughby's letter to Mr. Gripe, asking him to seek out his cousin, Letitia Slighcarp, as an instructress for his daughter and so—and so—"

"And so you conspired with Miss Slighcarp and forged her credentials," said Mr. Gripe angrily. "It is all very plain, sir! Take him away, gentlemen! Take him away and keep him fast until he can appear before a magistrate."

"After that it was very dull," said Bonnie, reporting the scene to Sylvia later. "I had to tell the Bow Street officers every single thing I could remember that Miss Slighcarp had done, and the clerk wrote it all down, and Mr. Gripe looked more and more shocked, especially when I told what I had seen when we looked through the hole in the secret panel and watched them tearing up Papa's will and all the other documents.

"And the end of it all is, Sylvia, that Mr. Grimshaw is committed to prison until the Assizes, when he will stand his trial for fraud, and the Bow Street officers are to go to Willoughby tomorrow to seize Miss Slighcarp!"

"How surprised she will be!" exclaimed Sylvia with lively pleasure. "I almost wish I could be there to see!"

"But, Sylvia, you are to be there! They most particularly requested that you and I should be taken too, to act as witnesses."

"But who will look after Aunt Jane?" inquired Sylvia anxiously.

"Dr. Field has said that he would procure a nurse for a few days. And it need be for only two—you can return directly Miss Slighcarp is apprehended. And Sylvia, as soon as Aunt Jane is well enough to travel, I have asked Mr. Gripe to arrange that she shall come and live at Willoughby, and be our guardian."

"Oh *yes!*" exclaimed Sylvia, her face brightening, "what a splendid plan, Bonnie!"

It was a gay and lively party that assembled in the train next day—very different from that earlier and sorrowful departure when Sylvia had taken leave of Aunt Jane. A special coupé compartment had been chartered, and the Bow Street officers had no objection to Simon and his geese traveling in it as well. Dr. Field was remaining to keep an eye on Aunt Jane, but he bade the children a cordial farewell and invited them to come and sleep in his apartment again when they returned to take Aunt Jane to Willoughby. Mr. Gripe the lawyer was with them, and had given his clerk instructions to procure a luncheon hamper from which came the most savory smells. Sylvia smiled faintly as she thought of the other tiny food packet and Mr. Grimshaw's sumptuous jam-filled cakes.

"I suppose he only pretended to have forgotten who he was when the portmanteau fell on him," she said to Bonnie.

"So that he would be taken to Willoughby," said Bonnie, nodding. "How I wish that we had left him in the train!"

"Still, he did save me from the wolves."

There were no wolves to be seen on this journey. The packs had all retreated to the bleak north country, and the train ran through smiling pasture lands, all astir with sheep and lambs, or through green and golden woods carpeted with bluebells.

The day passed gaily, with songs and storytelling—even the dry Mr. Gripe proved to know a number of amusing tales—and in between the laughter and chat Cardigan and Spock, the Bow Street officers, busily wrote down in their notebooks more and more of the dreadful deeds of Miss Slighcarp recounted to them by Bonnie and Sylvia.

They reached Willoughby Station at dawn. Mr. Gripe

had written to one of the inns at Blastburn for a chaise and it was there to meet them.

"How different this road seems," said Sylvia, as they set off at a gallop. "Last time I traveled along it there were wolves and snow and it was cold and dark—now I can see primroses everywhere and I am so hot in these clothes that I can hardly breathe."

They were still wearing the tinker children's clothes Pattern had made them, for there had been no time in London to get any others made. Mr. Gripe's eye winced when it encountered them, for he liked children to look neat and nicely dressed.

"Let us hope that Miss Slighcarp has not got rid of all our own clothes," said Bonnie.

When they reached the boundary of Willoughby Park they saw an enormous notice, new since they had left. It said:

WILLOUGHBY CHASE SCHOOL
A select Seminary for the Daughters of Gentlemen and the Nobility
Boarders and Parlor Boarders
Principals: MISS L. SLIGHCARP AND MRS. BRISKET

"What impertinence!" gasped Bonnie. "Can she really have made our home into a school?"

"This is worse even than I had feared," said Mr. Gripe grimly, as the chaise turned into the gateway.

They took the longer and more roundabout road that led to the back of the house, for the Bow Street officers wanted to surprise Miss Slighcarp.

"Didn't you say there was a secret passage, miss?" Sam Cardigan said to Bonnie.

"Yes, and a priests' hole and an oubliette—"

"Very good. Couldn't be better. We'll put some ginger in the good lady's gravy."

He explained his plan to Mr. Gripe and the children, and then they knocked at the back door. It was opened by James.

"Miss Bonnie! Miss Sylvia!" he exclaimed, scarlet with joy and surprise. They both flung themselves on him and hugged him.

"James, dear James! Are you all right? Is Pattern all right? What is going on here?"

"Terrible doings, miss—"

"Now, now," said Sam Cardigan. "Pleasure at seeing old acquaintance all very well, but business is business. We must get under cover. My man, where can this carriage be concealed?"

"It can go in the coach house, sir," James told him. "There's only Miss Slighcarp's landau now."

The carriage was hastily put away, and the conspirators took refuge in the dairy.

"Now James," said Bonnie, dancing with excitement, "you must go and tell Miss Slighcarp that Sylvia and I have come back, and that we are *very* sad and sorry for having run away. Don't say anything about these gentlemen."

"Yes, miss," said James, his eyes beginning to twinkle. "She's teaching just now, up in the schoolroom. The pupils study for an hour before breakfast."

"Is the entrance to the secret passage still open, James? Has Miss Slighcarp ever discovered it?"

"No to the second and yes to the first, Miss Bonnie," said James, and pulled aside the cupboard and horse blankets which he had arranged to conceal the opening.

"Capital! Go to her quickly, then, James! Tell her we are starving!"

"You don't look it, begging your pardon, miss," said James, grinning, and left the room. Mr. Gripe and the two

Bow Street officers squeezed their way into the secret passage. Simon, who had left his geese in the stable yard, hesitated, but Mr. Gripe said, "Come on, come on, boy. The more witnesses, the better," so he followed.

Bonnie and Sylvia spent the time while they waited for James's return in artistically dirtying and untidying each other, rubbing dust and coal on their faces, rumpling their hair, and making themselves look as dejected and orphanly as possible.

James came back with a long face.

"You're to come up to the schoolroom, young ladies. At once."

He led the way, and they followed in silence. The house bore traces everywhere of its new use as a school. On the crystal chandelier in the ballroom ropes had been slung for climbing, and the billiards table had been exchanged for blackboards. The portraits of ancestors in the long gallery had been replaced by bulletin boards and the gold-leaf and ormolu tables were covered with chalk powder and ink-stains.

Even though they knew they had good friends close at hand, the children could not control a certain swelled and breathless feeling in the region of their midriffs as they approached the schoolroom door.

James tapped at the door and in response to Miss Sligh-carp's "Come in" opened it and stood aside to let the children through.

A quick glance showed them that all the furniture had been removed and that the room was filled with desks. The more senior children from Mrs. Brisket's school were sitting at them, with expressions varying from nervous excitement to petrifaction on their faces.

Miss Slighcarp stood on a raised platform by a black-board. She had a long wooden pointer in her hand. Mrs.

Brisket was there, too, sitting at the instructress's desk. She wore a stern and forbidding expression, but on Miss Sligh-carp's face there was a look of triumph.

"So!" she said—a long, hissing exhalation. "So, you have returned!—Come here."

They advanced, slowly and trembling, until they stood below the platform. Miss Slighcarp was so tall that they had almost to lean back to look up at her.

"P-please take us back into your school, Miss Slighcarp," faltered Bonnie. "We're so cold and tired and hungry."

Into Sylvia's mind came a sudden recollection of the grouse pies and apricots they had eaten on the train. She bit her lip, and tried to look sorrowful.

Behind them, James quietly poked the fire, but no one noticed him. All eyes were on the returning truants.

"Hungry!" said Miss Slighcarp. "You'll be hungrier still before I've done with you. Do you think you can run away, spend two months idling and playing on the moors, return when it suits you, and then expect to be given roast beef and pudding? You'll have no food for three days! Perhaps that will teach you something. And you shall both be beaten, and we'll see what a taste of the dungeons will do for your spirit. James, go and get the dungeon keys."

"No, miss," said James firmly. "I obey some of your orders because I've got no alternative, but help to put children in those dungeons I can't and won't. It's not Christian." And he left the room, shutting the door sharply behind him.

"I'll get the keys, Letitia," said Mrs. Brisket, rising ponderously. "You can be administering chastisement, meanwhile."

Miss Slighcarp came down from her platform. "Miss Green," she said, and her eyes were so glittering with fury that even Bonnie quailed, "put out your hand."

Bonnie took a step backward. Miss Slighcarp followed

her, and raised the pointer menacingly. The children at the desks drew a tremulous breath. But just as the pointer came swishing down, the chimneypiece panel flew open, and Mr. Gripe, stepping out, seized hold of Miss Slighcarp's arm.

For a moment she was utterly dumfounded. Then, in wrath she exclaimed:

"Who are you, sir? Let me go at once! What are you doing in my house?"

"In your house, ma'am? In *your* house? Don't you remember me, Miss Slighcarp?" said Mr. Gripe. "I was the attorney instructed by your distant relative, Sir Willoughby Green, to seek you out and offer you the position of instructress to his daughter. You brought with you a testimonial from the Duchess of Kensington. Don't you remember?"

Miss Slighcarp turned pale.

"And who gave you permission, woman," suddenly thundered Mr. Gripe, "to turn this house into a boarding school? Who said you could use these children with villainous cruelty, beat them, starve them, and lock them in dungeons? Oh, its of no use to protest, I've been behind that panel and heard every word you've uttered."

"It was only a joke," faltered Miss Slighcarp. "I had no intention of really shutting them in the dungeons."

At this moment Mrs. Brisket re-entered the room holding a bunch of enormous rusty keys.

"We can't use the upper dungeons, Letitia," she began briskly, "for Lucy and Emma are occupying them. I have brought the lower . . ."

Then she saw Mr. Gripe, and behind him the two Bow Street officers. Her jaw dropped, and she was stricken to silence.

"Only a joke, indeed?" said Mr. Gripe harshly. "Mr. Cardigan, place these two females under arrest, if you please. Until it is convenient to remove them to jail, you may as well avail yourself of the dungeon keys so obligingly put at your disposal."

"You can't do this! You've no right!" shrieked the enraged Miss Slighcarp, struggling in the grip of Cardigan. "I have papers signed by Sir Willoughby empowering me to do as I please with this property in the event of his death, and appointing me guardian of the children—"

"Papers signed by Sir Willoughby. Pish!" said Mr. Gripe scornfully. "You may as well know, ma'am, that your accomplice Grimshaw, who is already in prison, has confessed to the whole plot."

At this news all the fight went out of Mrs. Brisket, and she allowed herself to be manacled by Spock, only muttering, "Grimshaw's a fool, a paltry, whining fool."

But Miss Slighcarp still gave battle.

"I tell you," she shouted, "I saw Sir Willoughby before he departed and he himself left me full powers—"

At this moment a heavy tread resounded along the passage, and they heard a voice exclaiming:

"What the *devil's* all this? Desks, blackboards, carpet taken up—has m'house been turned into a reformatory?"

The door burst open and in marched—Sir Willoughby Green! Behind him stood James, grinning for joy.

Bonnie turned absolutely pale with incredulity, stood so for a moment, motionless and wide-eyed, then, uttering one cry—*"Papa!"*—she flung herself into her father's arms.

"Well, minx? Have you missed us, eh? Have you been a good girl and minded your book? I can see you haven't," he said, surveying her lovingly. "Rosy as a pippin and brown as a berry. I can see you've been out of doors all day long instead of sewing your sampler and learning your *je ne sais quoi.* And Sylvia too—eh, my word, what a change from the little white mouse we left here! Well, well, well, girls will be girls! But what's all this, ma'am," he continued, addressing Miss Slighcarp threateningly, "what's all this hugger-mugger? I never gave you permission to turn Willoughby Chase into a school, no, damme I didn't! Being my fourth cousin doesn't give you such rights as that."

"But sir," interjected Mr. Gripe, who, at first silent with amazement, had now got his breath back, "Sir Willoughby! This is joyful indeed! We had all supposed you drowned when the *Thessaly* sank."

Sir Willoughby burst into a fit of laughter.

"Ay, so they told me at your office. We have been traveling close behind you, Mr. Gripe—I visited your place of business yesterday, learned you had just departed for Willoughby, and, since Lady Green was anxious to get back as soon as may be, and relieve the children's anxiety, we hired a special train and came posthaste after you."

"But were you not in the shipwreck then, Sir Willoughby?"

The reply to this question was lost in Bonnie's rapturous cry—"Is Mamma here too? *Is* she?"

"Why yes, miss, and ettling to see you, I'll be bound!"

Before the words had left his mouth Bonnie was out of the door. Sylvia, from a nice sense of delicacy, did not follow her cousin. She thought that Bonnie and her mother should be allowed those first few blissful moments of reunion alone together.

Sir Willoughby and Mr. Gripe had retired to a corner of the schoolroom and Mr. Gripe was talking hard, while Sir Willoughby listened with his blue eyes bulging, occasionally exclaiming, "Why damme! For sheer, cool, calm, impertinent effrontery—why, bless my soul!" Once he wheeled round to his niece and said, "Is it really true, Sylvia? Did Miss Slighcarp do these things?"

"Yes, sir, indeed she did," said Sylvia.

"Then hanging's too good for you, ma'am," he growled at Miss Slighcarp. "Have her taken to the dungeons, Gripe. When these two excellent fellows have breakfasted they can take her and the other harpy off to prison."

"Oh sir . . ." said Sylvia.

"Well, miss puss?"

"May I go with them to the dungeons, sir? I believe there are two children who have been put down there by Miss Slighcarp, and they will be so cold and unhappy and frightened!"

"Are there, by Joshua! We'll all go," said Sir Willoughby.

Sylvia had never visited the dungeons at Willoughby Chase. They were a dismal and frightening quarter, never entered by the present owner and his family, though in days gone by they had been extensively employed by ancestors of Sir Willoughby.

Down dark, dank, weed-encrusted steps they trod, and along narrow, rock-hewn passages, where the only sound beside the echo of their own footfalls was the drip of water. Sylvia shuddered when she remembered Miss Slighcarp's expressed intention of imprisoning herself and Bonnie down here.

"Oh, do let us hasten," she implored. "Poor Lucy and Emma must be nearly frozen with cold and fear."

"Upon my soul," muttered Mr. Gripe. "This passes everything. Fancy putting children in a place like this!"

Miss Slighcarp and Mrs. Brisket trod along in the rear of their captors, silent and sullen, looking neither to right nor to left.

The plight of Lucy and Emma was not quite so bad as it might have been. This was owing to the kindhearted James, who, though he could not release them, had contrived to pass through their bars a number of warm blankets and a quantity of kindling and some tapers, to enable them to light a fire, and he had also kept them supplied with food out of his own meagre rations.

But they were cold and miserable enough, and their astonishment and joy at the sight of Sylvia was touching to behold.

Sylvia danced up and down outside the bars with impatience while James found the right key, and then she hurried them off upstairs, without waiting to see Miss Slighcarp locked in their place.

"Come, come quickly, and get warm by a fire. Pattern shall make you a posset—or no, I forget, Pattern is probably not here yet, but I think I know how it is done."

However, they had no more than reached the Great Hall when they were greeted with an ecstatic cry from Bonnie.

"Sylvia! Emma! Lucy! Come and see Mamma! Oh, she is so different! So much better!"

They went rather shyly into the salon, where Pattern, who had been summoned by Simon at full gallop on one of the coach horses, bustled about in joyful tears and served everybody with cups of frothing hot chocolate.

"Well," a gay voice exclaimed, "where's my second daughter?" And in swept someone whom Sylvia would hardly have recognized for the frail, languid Lady Green, so blooming, beautiful, and bright-eyed did she appear. She embraced Sylvia, cordially made welcome the two poor prisoners, and declared:

"Now I want to hear all your story, every word, from the very beginning! I am proud of you both—and as for that Miss Slighcarp, cousin of your father's though she be, I hope she is sent to Botany Bay!"

"But Aunt Sophy," said Sylvia, "your tale must be so much more adventurous than ours! Were you not ship-wrecked?"

"Yes, indeed we were!" said Lady Green laughing, "and your uncle and I spent six very tedious days drifting in a rowing boat, our only fare being a monotonous choice of grapes or oranges, of which there happened to be a large crate in the dinghy, fortunately for us. We were then picked up by a small and *most* insanitary fishing boat, manned by a set of fellows as picturesque as they were un-washed, who none of them spoke a word of English. They would carry us nowhere but to their home port, which turned out to be the Canary Islands. On *this* boat we re-ceived nothing to eat but sardines in olive oil. I am sur-prised these shocks and privations did not carry me off, but Sir Willoughby maintains they were the saving of me, for from the time of the wreck my health began to pick up. On reaching the Canaries we determined to come home by the next mail ship, but they only visit these islands every three months or so, and one had just left. We had to wait a weary time, but the peace and the sunshine during our enforced stay completed my cure, as you see."

"Oh, how glad I am you came home and didn't go on round the world!" cried Bonnie.

Sir Willoughby marched in, beaming. "Well, well," he said, "has Madam Hen found her chicks, eh? But as for the state your house is in, my lady, I hardly dare describe it to you. We shall have to have it completely redecorated. And what's to be done with all these poor orphans?"

"Oh Papa," said Bonnie, bursting with excitement. "I have a plan for them!"

"You have, have you, hussy? What is it, then?"

"Don't you think Aunt Jane could come and live in the Dower House, just across the park, and run a school for them? Aunt Jane loves children!"

"What, Aunt Jane run a school? At her age?"

"Aunt Jane is very independent," Bonnie said. "She wouldn't want to feel she was living on charity. But she could have people to help her—*kind* people. And she could teach the girls beautiful embroidery!"

Lucy and Emma looked so wistful at the thought of this bliss that Sir Willoughby promised to consider it.

A happy party sat down to dine in the Great Hall that night. Spock and Cardigan, the Bow Street officials, had already left to commit their prisoners to the nearest jail, and the ruffianly gang of servants kept on by Miss Slighcarp had been summarily dismissed. Simon, riding about the countryside, had taken the news of Sir Willoughby's return to all the old servants, Solly and Timon and John Groom and Mrs. Shubunkin, and they had come hastening back.

The orphans, still dazed at their good fortune, sat at a table of their own, eating roast turkey and kindly averting their gaze from the pale cheeks and red eyes of Diana Brisket, who, having been in a position to bully and hector as much as she pleased, was now reduced to a state where she had not a friend to stand by her. Mrs. Brisket had sold the school in Blastburn and so Diana had nowhere to go and was forced, willy-nilly, to stay with the orphans (where, it may be said in passing, wholesome discipline and the example of Aunt Jane's unselfish nature soon wrought an improvement in her character). Some of the parlor boarders and daughters of the nobility and gentry had been fetched away by their parents, such as lived near enough, and the rest were awaiting removal.

Simon sat between Bonnie and Sylvia. Sir Willoughby gave him some very kindly looks. He had heard by now of Simon's brave part in rescuing the girls both from the wolves and from Mrs. Brisket's dreadful establishment, and of help with Aunt Jane's illness. The money he had spent had been returned to him with interest.

"It looks as if we're going to have an adopted son as well as an adopted daughter," said Sir Willoughby. "Hey, my boy? What shall we do with you, then? Put you through school?"

"No thank you, Sir Willoughby," said Simon gratefully but firmly. "School wouldn't suit me at all."

"What then? Can't just run wild."

"I'm going to be a painter," Simon explained. "Dr. Field said I showed great promise, and he told me I could stay with him and go to one of the famous London art schools."

"Oh Simon," said Bonnie, dismayed, "and leave Willoughby?"

"I'll come back every holidays," he told her. "Remember we promised to go and see Mr. Wilderness? I want to paint a picture of Great Whinside from the dale—oh, and a hundred other places round here."

"Sensible lad," approved Sir Willoughby. "Well, always remember, whenever you come back, there's a warm welcome for you at Willoughby Chase."

"Thank you, Sir Willoughby," said Simon beaming. "And now if you'll excuse me, I think I ought to be returning to my cave. I want to see how my bees are getting on."

"Good night, Simon," cried Bonnie and Sylvia, "we shall come and see you tomorrow."

Bonnie yawned.

"It's long past these children's bedtime," said Sir Willoughby, "and they were traveling all night. Off with you now—I dare say your mother will be up by and by to say good night to you in bed."

Their own room had been hastily prepared for them and they were glad to tumble between the fine silken sheets. "And oh, Bonnie," called Sylvia, "*have* you seen the pretty dresses Pattern has been making for us?"

"I've grown accustomed to boys' clothes," grumbled Bonnie.

"Oh, what nonsense, miss!" said Pattern scoldingly, and ruined the effect by giving Bonnie a hug. "There now, go to sleep, you blessed pair, and don't let either of you move a muscle till you're called. We've had quite enough to worry about today, with everything at sixes and sevens, and no servants to speak of, and a hundred orphans to feed. Mind! You're not to speak a word till eight o'clock. You're not even to dream!"

"Dream," murmured Bonnie sleepily, "we can't help dreaming, Pattern. We've so much to dream *about*—the wolves, and Miss Slighcarp, and walking to London, and helping poor Aunt Jane, and Mamma and Papa adrift in a boat full or oranges and grapes . . ." Her voice trailed away into sleep.

Light after light in the windows of the great house was

extinguished, until at length it stood dark and silent. And though the house had witnessed many strange scenes, wolf hunts and wine drinking and weddings and wars, it is doubtful whether during its whole history any of its inmates had had such adventures as those of Sylvia and Bonnie Green.

ABOUT THE AUTHOR:

Author Joan Aiken, daughter of American writer Conrad Aiken, was born in Rye, Sussex, England. She has engaged in a variety of work, including ten years with the London office of the United Nations. For five years she was a features editor for *Argosy*, and more recently has worked as a copywriter for a large London advertising agency. Now she devotes all her time to free-lance authorship. Her hobbies are painting and gardening at her home, an ex-pub in Petworth, England, where she lives with her two teen-age children.

ABOUT THE ILLUSTRATOR:

Artist Pat Marriott was born in Cheshire and grew up in London, England. She studied at the Westminster School of Art and at Chelsea School of Art. She is now a free-lance artist and was the illustrator for *The Mystery of the Polly Harris,* a Doubleday Book for Young Readers.